PUFFIN BOOKS

This Little Puffin

Elizabeth Matterson's interest in songs for young children arises from extensive and intensive work with the people who care for young children – as an NNEB course tutor, a playgroup course tutor and as a tutor to courses for childminders and parents – and from direct experience with young children as a playgroup leader and her work with children and families who have special needs.

Her other writing projects include the book *Play with a Purpose for Under-Sevens*, which was made into a TV series.

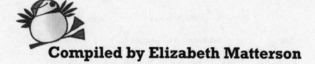

Compiled by Elizabeth Matterson

This Little Puffin

Music arrangements by
Elizabeth Matterson and Sue Whitham

Illustrated by Claudio Muñoz

Diagrams by David Woodroffe

PUFFIN

PUFFIN BOOKS

Published by the Penguin Group
Penguin Books Ltd, 80 Strand, London WC2R 0RL, England
Penguin Group (USA) Inc., 375 Hudson Street, New York, New York 10014, USA
Penguin Group (Canada), 90 Eglinton Avenue East, Suite 700, Toronto, Ontario, Canada M4P 2Y3
(a division of Pearson Penguin Canada Inc.)
Penguin Ireland, 25 St Stephen's Green, Dublin 2, Ireland (a division of Penguin Books Ltd)
Penguin Group (Australia), 250 Camberwell Road, Camberwell, Victoria 3124, Australia
(a division of Pearson Australia Group Pty Ltd)
Penguin Books India Pvt Ltd, 11 Community Centre, Panchsheel Park, New Delhi – 110 017, India
Penguin Group (NZ), 67 Apollo Drive, Rosedale, North Shore 0632, New Zealand
(a division of Pearson New Zealand Ltd)
Penguin Books (South Africa) (Pty) Ltd, 24 Sturdee Avenue, Rosebank, Johannesburg 2196, South Africa

Penguin Books Ltd, Registered Offices: 80 Strand, London WC2R 0RL, England

puffinbooks.com

First published 1969
This revised edition, with new illustrations published 1991

33

Copyright © Elizabeth Matterson, 1969, 1991
Music arrangements copyright © Elizabeth Matterson and Sue Whitham, 1991
Illustrations copyright © Claudio Muñoz, 1991
Diagrams copyright © David Woodroffe, 1969
All rights reserved

The moral right of the author and illustrators has been asserted
The acknowledgements on pages 319–321 constitute an extension of this copyright page

Filmset in Bembo
Made and printed in England by Clays Ltd, St Ives plc

British Library Cataloguing in Publication Data
A CIP catalogue record for this book is available from the British Library

ISBN: 978-0-140-34048-8

www.greenpenguin.co.uk

Penguin Books is committed to a sustainable future
for our business, our readers and our planet.
The book in your hands is made from paper
certified by the Forest Stewardship Council.

Contents

Introduction

There are many good reasons for using music and rhymes with young children. The first and most important reason is that most children and adults enjoy it enormously. If we need more justification than that then it provides excellent speech practice and voice control – some children who have speech difficulties actually find it easier to sing than to talk. Although many rhymes and songs are simple in content they increase vocabulary, and the repeated patterns and sequences of words and rhythm are good memory exercises. The ritual of taking turns and conforming to the 'rules', and the communication there can be in sharing an experience which crosses both age and cultural gaps, are useful factors in social development.

At home there is a limit to the amount of meaningful, direct conversation that is possible with very young children. Songs and rhymes provide non-demanding communication and create a happy and relaxed activity. Most households develop their own repertoire of bedtime and silly-time songs. There are other times when singing can distract a frightened child, change the mood of a fretful child and can while away tedious experiences such as journeys or waiting times when no other activity is possible. In terms of resources it costs nothing, needs no equipment and can be done anywhere.

A repertoire of well-known baby songs and nursery rhymes and the familiarity of singing with others is a very useful attribute for a child to take with him when he first joins a group, whether his first experience is with a child-minder, in a Mother and Baby group, Parent and Toddler group, play group, nursery class or school. A skilful leader can use what the child already knows and build on this to develop his confidence that some things are still the same in this new situation. Similarly, songs learned in the play group or nursery class can be built on in the infant school.

In groups for under-fives, 'music' is just about the only activity that everyone does at the same time. This helps to create a group identity and also enables children to get to know others and to be known. The new songs and games children take home are a valuable link between home and group – even the child who sits quietly and doesn't sing a word will often go home and sing the song she did not appear to know in the group. This is one of the great advantages of music as an activity . . . everyone can join in at their own level and their own pace, whether it is just listening, clapping hands or doing simple actions, saying the last word of a line, singing the chorus, singing all of the song with everyone else, insisting on singing the song *to* everyone else and expecting applause at the end, or right through to the ultimate stage of making up new words and different versions to add to a song.

As for the adults who sing with children – most of us freely admit that we have no special musical talent and are not particularly good at singing. We simply learn the tune by what most people refer to as 'picking it up' and then, without wondering about the musical niceties, automatically transpose it into a key that suits us and with which we feel comfortable. Even for those people who do play a musical instrument, it is one thing to play well when all one's attention can be given to the piece being played – and quite another to have enough ability and confidence for the playing to be a second nature skill which leaves the player free to give the undivided attention and concentration, plus the use of eyes, ears, hands, voice and that special sixth sense which is needed to create a rapport both with and within the group. What we do need, however, like the children, is a repertoire of tried and tested songs.

The material for the first edition of *This Little Puffin* was collected twenty-five years ago with the help of nursery school teachers, nursery nurses and play group leaders who generously shared their children's favourite songs – and nobly copied them out, provided the music and, where possible, traced the origin of the songs. This collection has survived extremely well. Every one of the songs is still being used somewhere by someone and some have become classic items appearing in every nursery group list of favourites.

The recent survey carried out to provide an updated edition has been based on a much wider spread of users of music with young children. It included some group leaders of the Mother and Baby groups, Mother and Toddler groups, pre-school music groups and Day Centres which did not exist twenty-five years ago . . . plus mothers, child-minders, groups for children with special needs . . . in addition to play groups, nursery classes, nursery schools and infant schools, including some where the children come from mixed ethnic backgrounds. It also crossed the generation gap in that some of the material was indirectly provided by Grannies and Grandads. The area covered included Orkney and the Shetland Isles to the north, the Isle of Wight and Cornwall to the south, and from the east coast of Norfolk to the west coast of Northern Ireland.

This generation of contributors have worked just as hard and willingly as their predecessors and between us we have come up with a glorious mixture of action songs, games, finger plays and rhymes which should last until the present generation of children are old enough to become contributors in their turn. The survey has also turned up some interesting and useful information on how people learn the songs they sing with children, and when and how they are used, but that is another story.

Another aspect which has been explored is the changes there have been in the repertoires of specific groups in specific places over the last quarter of a century. With a great deal of patient help from some of those nursery schools and infant schools which have survived to be involved in both collections, it is possible to see both differences and similarities in their lists. Most of the 1969 favourites are still popular . . . but the general trend is to use the more flexible, adaptable songs which can be presented in different ways to give them spontaneous relevance to what is important in the group at any one time. There are less of the rigid, subject specific, music specific songs and some which might now be labelled rather 'twee' seem to be rarely used. The picture is of more willingness to adapt, of greater freedom and of more participation by the children, and this is borne out by an overall comparison of the two collections.

Thanks are due to everyone who helped, whether by providing lists of songs, writing out music, checking sources or providing information about their family situation or what happens in what kind of group, or by giving permission for their original work and ideas to be used ... and in many cases by providing all of these. The enthusiasm and enjoyment that these adults share with their children for singing together is self evident.

Very special thanks are due to Sue Whitham MA Cantab who proved a tower of strength in checking and preparing the melody lines. Her brief was to provide just enough 'user-friendly' music to enable anyone to learn the tune for a song, in a key that was comfortable for most adults and children to sing. Since quite a number of people mentioned guitars and keyboards she has provided just enough chords for those 'would-be' or 'only-just' guitar or keyboard players to have a go at providing a cheerful accompaniment without denting their confidence by demanding too much expertise. There are even some songs where one can get by with just one chord throughout which should encourage any beginner. In some cases she has indicated use of a capo for the guitar (a simple and definitely cheating device which raises the tone of the strings) to avoid the need for some of the more difficult fingering. Obviously her own professional training and qualification helped ... but the fact that she has three young children, her experience of running a music group for young children and helping with music activities for rather older children in school, and the undoubted bonus of having a mother who was involved with music for young children, were all equally valuable.

Checking sources and copyright of songs and rhymes has been even more difficult this time than it was last time even with the help of many pairs of eyes. There are now more publishers taking an interest in this field and a number of music producers have issued tapes of songs for children. The origins of the songs and rhymes used have not always been acknowledged and therefore the issue has become even more confused. Every effort has been made to establish the original copyright of items and thanks are due to those authors, composers and publishers who have given permission for copyright material to be included. The best songs and rhymes, however, tend to be passed on in the manner of folk-song with the slight changes and extra verses that are inevitable. More often than not contributors may re-member who passed a song on to them but do not know where *that* person learned it. If any omissions have been made please let us know and we will make appropriate acknowledgement in the next edition.

Elizabeth Matterson

1 Baby Games

Hands, Feet and Faces

This little pig went to market,
This little pig stayed at home;
This little pig had roast beef,
This little pig had none.
This little pig cried, 'Wee-wee-wee,
I can't find my way home.'

*Point to each toe in turn, starting with the big one,
and on the last line tickle underneath the baby's foot.*

This little cow eats grass,
This little cow eats hay;
This little cow drinks water,
This little cow runs away;
This little cow does nothing
But just lies down all day.
We'll chase her,
We'll chase her,
We'll chase her away!

Point to each finger in turn, starting with the thumb.
Tickle the little finger and then up the baby's arm.

Knock at the door,

> *Pretend to knock on the forehead.*

Pull the bell,
> *Lightly pull a lock of hair.*

Lift the latch,

> *Lightly pinch the nose.*

And walk in.
> *Pretend to put your fingers on his mouth.*

Use this as a feature play with a baby.

Pat-a-cake, pat-a-cake,
Baker's man,
Bake me a cake
As fast as you can.
Pat it and prick it
And mark it with B,
And put it in the oven
For Baby and me.

Use this for a hand-clapping game with a baby.
Use the traditional tune.

Shoe a little horse,
Shoe a little mare,
But let the little colt
Go bare, bare, bare.

Say this rhyme while patting a baby's feet.

Tickly Rhymes

Slowly, slowly, very slowly
Creeps the garden snail.
Slowly, slowly, very slowly
Up the wooden rail.

Quickly, quickly, very quickly
Runs the little mouse.
Quickly, quickly, very quickly
Round about the house.

*Use hands to mime the actions suggested by the words,
or play with the baby as a tickling game.*

Round and round the garden
Run your index finger round the baby's palm
Went the Teddy Bear,
One step,
Two steps,
'Jump' your finger up his arm.
Tickly under there.
Tickle him under his arm.

Round and round the haystack
Went the little mouse,
One step,
Two steps,
In his little house.

Repeat the same actions for the second verse.

Peep-Bo Games

Peek-a-boo, Peek-a-boo,
Who's that hiding there?
Peek-a-boo, Peek-a-boo,
(Peter)'s behind the chair!

Peek-a-boo, Peek-a-boo,
I see you hiding there!
Peek-a-boo, Peek-a-boo,
Come from behind the chair!

The toddler hides away and an adult 'finds' him.
Smaller tots who are not able to hide themselves can
be hidden by another adult or an older brother
or sister.

Capo 1st fret for chords in brackets

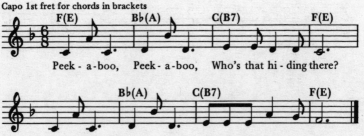

Clap–a–clap–a–handies,
(Teddy)'s come to play;
Cover up your little eyes
Help the child cover his eyes.
While he hides away!

Where's Teddy?
Where's Teddy?
BOO!

EMM et al.

Chant this last part. It could equally well be
Daddy, Mummy, Granny, etc. who hides, or a different
toy which is hidden.

Capo 1st fret for chords in brackets

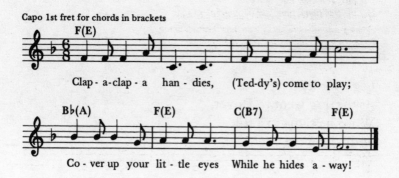

Knee and Shoulder Rides

Ride a cock horse
To Banbury Cross,
To see a fine lady
Upon a white horse.
With rings on her fingers
And bells on her toes,
She shall have music
Wherever she goes.

Use this for a knee ride for a baby.
Use the traditional tune.

Leg over leg
As the dog went to Dover,
When he came to a stile –
Jump, he went over.

Cross your knees and sit the baby on one ankle, holding his hands.
Bounce him to the rhythm of the rhyme, and on 'Jump' give him a big
swing by uncrossing your knees.

Trot, trot, trot,
Go and never stop.
Trudge along, my little pony,
Where 'tis rough and where 'tis stony.
Go and never stop,
Trot, trot, trot, trot, trot!

*Use this for a knee ride for a baby, making the bounces fit in with the rhythm of
the rhyme.*

Trot, trot, trot, Go and ne-ver stop. Trudge a-long, my

lit - tle po - ny, Where 'tis rough and where 'tis sto - ny.

Go and ne-ver stop, Trot, trot, trot, trot, trot!

Going fishing in the deep blue sea,
> *Child sat astride the adult's knee, hands held firmly.*

Catching fishes for my tea;
> *Let him down slowly between knees so that his head hangs down.*

Catch another for my brother,
> *Give a little pull upwards.*

One! Two! Three!
> *Big pull upwards so that he comes upright on 'Three'.*

Capo 1st fret for chords in brackets

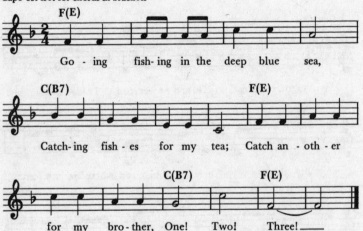

Go - ing fish- ing in the deep blue sea,
Catch- ing fish - es for my tea; Catch an - oth - er
for my bro - ther, One! Two! Three! ___

Walter, Walter, Wagtail

Bounce child astride adult's knee, hands held firmly.

Sat upon a pole;
He wagged his tail,

Move knees to left and right.

And wagged his tail,
Till he fell down a hole!

Open knees and let child slip down.

Music EMM et al.

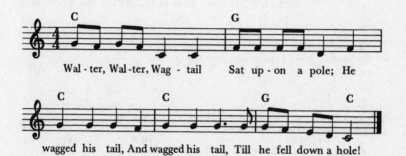

Wal-ter, Wal-ter, Wag-tail   Sat up-on a pole; He

wagged his tail, And wagged his tail, Till he fell down a hole!

Giddy up and away we go,
Riding on a donkey;
Giddy up and away we go,
Riding round the town!

Giddy up and away we go, etc.
Riding up the mountain!

Giddy up and away we go, etc.
Riding down the hill!

SHIRLEY DOWNS and ELIZABETH MATTERSON

The child sits on the adult's shoulders or 'piggyback'
fashion and is given a rather bouncy ride to anywhere
anyone likes to suggest.

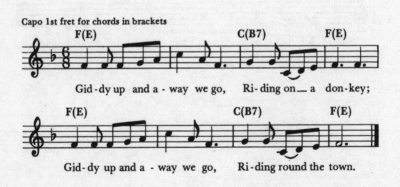

Capo 1st fret for chords in brackets

Gid-dy up and a-way we go, Ri-ding on— a don-key;

Gid-dy up and a-way we go, Ri-ding round the town.

Through the Day

What shall we do with a girl called (Katy)?
What shall we do with a girl called (Katy)?
What shall we do with a girl called (Katy)?
Ready for the day!

We'll wash her face until it's clean, etc.

We'll clean her teeth until they sparkle, etc.

We'll put her pants and socks and shoes on, etc.

We'll brush her hair until it shines, etc.

Then reverse and repeat the whole process at night . . .

What shall we do with a girl called (Katy)? etc.
When it comes to bedtime!

EMM et al.

This is sung to the tune of
What shall we do with the Drunken Sailor?

All the little milk teeth
Standing in a row,
Scrub, scrub, scrub,
And away we go.

First do all the front ones,
Then do at the back,
Every night and morning,
Just like that.

DIANA NEAL

*Use the tune of I had a Little Nut Tree to sing
this during teeth-cleaning sessions.*

Baby (Peter), Baby (Peter),
Where are you, where are you?
Sitting in your high chair,
Sitting in your high chair;
I see you,
Yes I do!

SHEILA GROVE

This is sung to the tune of Frère Jaques.

There are lots of other possibilities throughout the day
e.g. Lying on the changing mat.
      Sitting in the nice warm bath.
      Riding in the push chair.
      Sitting on your Mummy's knee.

This is the way we put on our coats,
Put on our coats, put on our coats;
This is the way we put on our coats,
When we're going shopping!

The possibilities are limitless, e.g.
Put on our wellies . . . To go out in the rain.
Put on our bibs . . . When it's time for tea.
Put on our mittens . . . When it's cold outside.
Put on our sun-hats . . . When the sun is too bright.

This is sung to the tune of Here we go round the Mulberry Bush
(see page 62).

She didn't dance, she didn't dance,
She didn't dance today;
She didn't dance, she didn't dance,
There was no one to play!

Hold the baby up and wriggle her gently.

So throw her up, so throw her up,
So throw her up on high;
So throw her up, so throw her up,
She'll come down by and by!

Pretend to throw the baby up in the air.

She didn't smile, she didn't smile,
She didn't smile today;
She didn't smile, she didn't smile,
Because no one could play!

So throw her up etc.

RACHEL WAKE'S GRANDMA

Bedtime

Up the wooden hill
To Bedfordshire;
And down Sheet Lane
To Blanket Fair.

*The wooden hill is the stairs and Sheet Lane
is getting in between the sheets.*

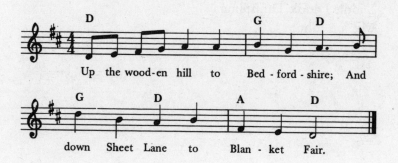

Goodnight Tommy, Goodnight Anne,
Goodnight children,
It's time to go to bed.

EMM et al.

*This is sung to the same tune as Goodbye (Peter), goodbye (Anne)
(see page 154).*

Diddle Diddle Dumpling,
My son John
Went to bed with his trousers on;
One shoe off and the other shoe on,
Diddle Diddle Dumpling,
My son John.

2 Nursery Rhymes and Variations

Baa Baa black sheep,
Have you any wool?
Yes sir, yes sir,
Three bags full.

One for the master,
One for the dame;
One for the little boy
Who lives down the lane.

Additional verse for babies:

'Thank you,' said the master,
'Thank you,' said the dame;
'Thank you,' said the little boy
Who lives down the lane.

Variations for slightly older children:

Baa Baa white sheep,
Have you any wool?
Yes sir, yes sir,
Three needles full.

One to mend a jumper,
One to mend a frock;
And one for the little boy
With holes in his socks.

Baa Baa grey sheep,
Have you any wool?
Yes sir, yes sir,
Three bags full.

One for the kittens,
One for the cats;
And one for the guinea pigs
To knit some woolly hats.

'Thank you,' etc.
We'd like some woolly hats!

JOAN CLAYTON AND THE LAWNS NURSERY SCHOOL

Ring-o-Ring-o-Roses, a pocket full of posies;
Atishoo, atishoo, we all fall down!

The King has sent his daughter, to fetch a pail of water;
Atishoo, atishoo, we all fall down!

The robin on the steeple is singing to the people
Atishoo, atishoo, we all fall down!

The cows are in the meadow, eating buttercups;
Atishoo, atishoo, we all jump up!

Fishes in the water, fishes in the sea;
We all jump up with a One! Two! Three!

Ashes in the water, ashes in the sea;
We all jump up with a One! Two! Three!

Swimmers' version:

Ring-o-Ring-o-Roses,
Water up our noses!
Atishoo, atishoo
But we won't drown.

An Irish version:

Daddy's in the milk jug,
Mummy's in the cup;
Baby's in the sugar bowl,
We all jump up!

Additional verses for another great favourite:

Hickory Dickory Dock,
The mouse ran up the clock;
The clock struck One,
The mouse ran down,
Hickory Dickory Dock!

Hickory Dickory Dock,
The mouse ran up the clock;
The clock struck Two,
The mouse said BOO!
Hickory Dickory Dock!

Hickory Dickory Dock,
The mouse ran up the clock;
The clock struck Three,
The mouse said Wheeeee . . .
As he slid down the clock!

GLENDA BANKS and ELIZABETH MATTERSON

Variation:

Hickory Dickory Dare,
The pig flew up in the air;
The man in the moon,
Sent him down quite soon,
Hickory Dickory Dare!

Humpty Dumpty sat on a wall,
Humpty Dumpty had a great fall;
All the King's horses and all the King's men
Couldn't put Humpty together again.

Nursery addition:

Along came the children
With brushes and glue,
And stuck Humpty together
As good as new!

Slightly dotty version which is widely used:

Humpty Dumpty sat up in bed
Eating yellow bananas;
Where do you think he put the skins?
Down his striped pyjamas!

An 'echo' variation as a singing game for older children:

First voice:	Humpty Dumpty sat on a wall,
Second voice:	(He sat on a wall.)
First:	Humpty Dumpty had a great fall;
Second:	(He had a great fall.)
First:	All the King's horses and all the King's men
Second:	(All of the horses and all of the men.)
First:	Couldn't put Humpty together again.
Second:	(Together again.)

EMM et al.

To market, to market to buy a fat pig,
Home again, home again, jiggetty jig.

To market, to market to buy a fat hog,
Home again, home again, jiggetty jog.

To market, to market to buy a plum bun
Home again, home again, market is done.

Variations:

To market, to market to buy an old hen,
Home again, home again, ricketty ren.

To market, to market to buy a young chick,
Home again, home again, ricketty rick.

Followed by:
Old sheep/ricketty reep
Young lamb/ricketty ramb
Old goat/ricketty roat
Young kid/ricketty rid

and whatever else the children suggest.

EMM et al.

When children know a rhyme well they will giggle if the wrong words are used and suggest variations themselves if invited, e.g.

Sing a song of sixpence,
A pocket full of rye;
Four and twenty blackbirds,
Baked in a pie;
When the pie was opened
The birds began to sing,
Wasn't that a dainty dish to set before the King?

Becomes:
Sing a song of (ten p)
A pocket full of (spaghetti)
Four and twenty (tadpoles), etc.

Polly put the kettle on,
Polly put the kettle on,
Polly put the kettle on,
We'll all have tea.

Variations:

Beans on toast and chocolate cake,
Beans on toast and chocolate cake,
Beans on toast and chocolate cake,
That's what we like for tea!

ELIZABETH MATTERSON

Plus any other suggestions the children like to make if they can fit them to the rhythm of the song.

3 Nursery Favourites

Finger Plays

Incy Wincy Spider climbed up the water spout,

Use the fingers of both hands to represent a spider climbing up.

Down came the raindrops and washed poor Incy out;

Raise the hands and lower them slowly, wriggling fingers to indicate rain.

Out came the sunshine and dried up all the rain,

Raise hands above the head together and bring them out and down.

And Incy Wincy Spider climbed up that spout again.

As first line.

In - cy Win - cy Spi - der climbed up the wa - ter spout,

Down came the rain - drops and washed poor In - cy out;

Out came the sun - shine and dried up all the rain, and

In - cy Win - cy Spi - der climbed up that spout a - gain.

Five little ducks went swimming one day,
Over the pond and far away.
Mother Duck said, 'Quack, quack, quack, quack,'
But only four little ducks came back.

Four little ducks went swimming one day, etc.

Last verse:
One little duck went swimming one day
Over the pond and far away.
Mother Duck said, 'Quack, quack, quack, quack,'
And five little ducks came swimming back.

WYN DANIEL EVANS

Use the fingers of one hand and wriggle them to represent the ducks swimming.

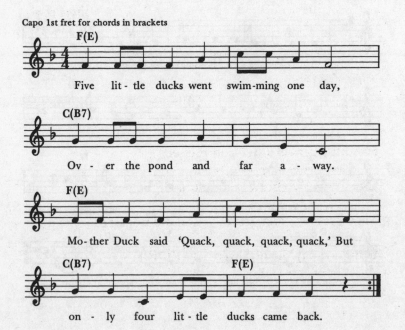

Capo 1st fret for chords in brackets

F(E)
Five lit - tle ducks went swim-ming one day,

C(B7)
Ov - er the pond and far a - way.

F(E)
Mo- ther Duck said 'Quack, quack, quack, quack,' But

C(B7)   F(E)
on - ly four lit - tle ducks came back.

Ten fat sausages sizzling in the pan,
Hold up fingers and thumbs of both hands.

One went POP! and another went BANG!
Finger in mouth to make a pop, clap hands loudly for bang.

Eight fat sausages, etc.
Hold up just fingers on each hand.

And eventually:
No fat sausages sizzling in the pan,
But, all of a sudden, the pan went Bang!
It went BANG! It went BANG!
It went BANG! BANG! BANG!
Now there are no sizzling sausages
And no frying pan!

EMM et al.

*This is usually chanted rather than sung but it can be fitted
to the tune of Ten Green Bottles if the first line of each verse
is repeated three times.*

Five little peas in a pea-pod pressed,
Clench fingers of one hand.

One grew, two grew, and so did all the rest;
Open out fingers slowly.

They grew . . . and grew . . . and did not stop,
Stretch fingers wide.

Until one day the pod went . . . POP!
Clap loudly on POP.

Tommy Thumb, Tommy Thumb,
Where are you?
Here I am, here I am,
How do you do?

Peter Pointer, Peter Pointer, etc.

Toby Tall, Toby Tall, etc.

Ruby Ring, Ruby Ring, etc.

Baby Small, Baby Small, etc.

Fingers All, Fingers All, etc.

Bring hands out from behind back after 'Where are you?'
1st verse: Wriggle both thumbs and make them bow on the last line.
2nd verse: Repeat, using index fingers.
3rd verse: Use middle fingers.
4th verse: Use ring fingers.
5th verse: Use little fingers.
6th verse: Use all fingers.

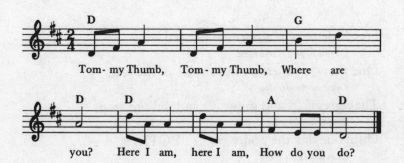

Two little dicky-birds sitting on a wall,
> *Use forefingers to represent birds.*

One named Peter, one named Paul;
> *Wriggle one finger for each bird.*

Fly away Peter, fly away Paul;
> *Put appropriate finger behind back.*

Come back Peter, come back Paul!
> *Fingers come back as they are named.*

Action Songs and Rhymes

Down by the station, early in the morning,
See the little puffer trains all in a row.
See the engine driver pull the little handle.
Choo, choo, choo, and off we go.

Down at the farmyard early in the morning,
See the little tractor standing in the barn.
Do you see the farmer pull the little handle?
Chug, chug, chug, and off we go.

Five currant buns in a baker's shop,
Round and fat with sugar on the top.
Along came a boy with a penny one day,
Bought a currant bun and took it away.

Four currant buns, etc.

This may be played with fingers or by having five children represent the buns and another child the boy with the penny.

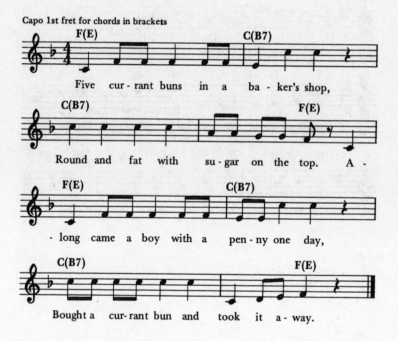

Capo 1st fret for chords in brackets

Five cur-rant buns in a ba-ker's shop,
Round and fat with su-gar on the top. A-
-long came a boy with a pen-ny one day,
Bought a cur-rant bun and took it a-way.

I'm a little teapot, short and stout;
> *Children make themselves stout.*

Here's my handle, here's my spout.
> *Put one hand on hip, hold out the other arm as a spout.*

When I see the teacups, hear me shout,
> *Stand as above.*

'Tip me up and pour me out.'
> *Tip slowly to the side of the outstretched arm.*

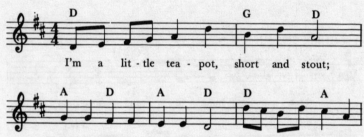

I'm a lit-tle tea-pot, short and stout;

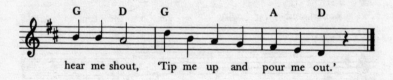

Here's my han-dle, here's my spout. When I see the tea-cups,

hear me shout, 'Tip me up and pour me out.'

I hear thunder, I hear thunder;
Drum the feet on the floor.

Hark, don't you, Hark, don't you?
Pretend to listen.

Pitter-patter raindrops,
Indicate rain with fingers.

Pitter-patter raindrops,
I'm wet through,
Shake the whole body vigorously.

SO ARE YOU!
Point to a neighbour.

I see blue skies, I see blue skies
Shade eyes and look up,

Way up high, way up high;
Reach up with arms.

Hurry up the sunshine,
Hunch shoulders and shiver.

Hurry up the sunshine
We'll soon dry,
Rub arms and legs vigorously.

We'll soon dry!

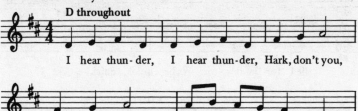

Miss Polly had a dolly who was sick, sick, sick.
  Fold arms and rock a pretend dolly.

So she called for the doctor to be quick, quick, quick;
  One hand to ear and one to mouth for telephone.

The doctor came with his bag and his hat,
  One hand swings bag and other holds hat on.

And he knocked on the door with a rat-a-tat-tat.
  Knock one fist on palm of other hand.

He looked at the dolly, and he shook his head,
  Shake head very gravely.

And he said, 'Miss Polly, put her straight to bed'.
  Shake finger.

He wrote on a paper for a pill, pill, pill,
  Write with finger on palm of other hand.

'That will make her better, yes it will, will, will!'
  Nod vigorously.

Capo 1st fret for chords in brackets

Row, row, row your boat,
Gently down the stream;
Merrily, merrily, merrily, merrily,
Life is but a dream.

Row, row, row your boat,
Gently out to sea;
Merrily, merrily, merrily, merrily,
We'll be home for tea.

Row, row, row your boat,
Gently on the tide;
Merrily, merrily, merrily, merrily,
To the other side.

Row, row, row your boat,
Gently back to shore;
Merrily, merrily, merrily, merrily,
Home for tea at four.

*Two children sit facing each other on the floor holding hands
and move first towards one child then the other.*

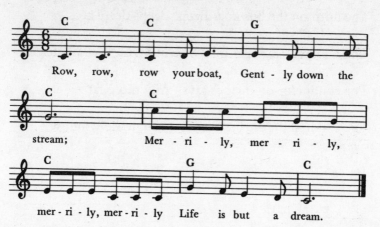

Up the tall white candlestick
Make left arm into candlestick.
Crept little Mousie Brown;
Two fingers of right hand run up the candlestick.
Right to the top, but he couldn't get down!
Fingers wriggle at the top.
So he called to his Grandma,
Call through cupped hands.
Grandma! Grandma!
But Grandma was in town . . .
So he curled himself into a ball –
And rolled himself right down.
Clench both fists and roly-poly them round each other.

The wheels on the bus go round and round,
Round and round, round and round;
The wheels on the bus go round and round,
All day long.

The horn on the bus goes Beep! Beep! Beep! etc.

The windscreen wiper goes Swish! Swish! Swish! etc.

The conductor on the bus says, 'Any more fares?' etc.

The children on the bus watch through the window,
etc.

The Mummies on the bus go 'Chat! Chat! Chat!' etc.

The Daddies on the bus go Nod, Nod, Nod! etc.

The babies on the bus fall fast asleep, etc.

The doggies on the bus go Woof! Woof! Woof! etc.

The old ladies on the bus say, 'Mind my toes, dear!' etc.

Other variations:
The wheels on the bus, etc.
All the way to (Hanley).
Or to London, the shops, the zoo, the seaside, Granny's house – wherever the children suggest.

EMM et al.

Mime the actions suggested by the words. Other situations may be suggested by the children.

Capo 1st fret for chords in brackets

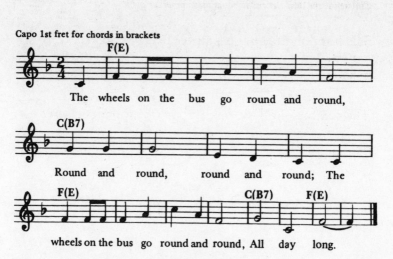

The wheels on the bus go round and round,
Round and round, round and round; The
wheels on the bus go round and round, All day long.

When all the cows were sleeping, and the sun had gone
  to bed,
Up jumped the scarecrow, and this is what he said:
'I'm a dingle-dangle scarecrow with a flippy, floppy hat.
I can shake my hands like this, and shake my feet like
  that!'

When all the hens were roosting, and the moon behind
  a cloud,
Up jumped the scarecrow, and shouted very loud:
'I'm a dingle-dangle scarecrow,' etc.

When the dogs were in the kennel, and the doves were
  in the loft,
Up jumped the scarecrow, and whispered very soft:
'I'm a dingle-dangle scarecrow,' etc.

M. RUSSELL-SMITH and G. RUSSELL-SMITH

Children shake their feet and hands at the appropriate point.

Little Peter Rabbit had a fly upon his nose,
Little Peter Rabbit had a fly upon his nose,
Little Peter Rabbit had a fly upon his nose,
So he flicked it and it flew away, away, away!

Little Peter Rabbit had an ant upon his ear, etc.
And it ran away, away, away!

Little Peter Rabbit had a butterfly on his paw, etc.
And it fluttered away, away, away!

The children will make other suggestions.
This is sung to the tune of John Brown's Tractor (see page 220).

Wind the bobbin up,
> *Roll fists round each other.*

Wind the bobbin up,
Pull, pull, clap, clap, clap;
> *Pull fists apart as though pulling elastic, then clap.*

Point to the ceiling,
> *Do the actions as they are mentioned.*

Point to the floor,
Point to the window,
Point to the door,
Clap your hands together,
One, two, three,
Put your hands upon your knee.

Wind the bob-bin up, Wind the bob-bin up,

Pull, pull, clap, clap, clap; Point to the ceil-ing,

Point to the floor, Point to the win-dow, Point to the door.

Clap your hands to-ge-ther, One, two, three,

Put your hands up - on your knee.

Singing Games

Here we go round the Mulberry Bush,
The Mulberry Bush, the Mulberry Bush,
Here we go round the Mulberry Bush
On a cold and frosty morning.

This is the way we sweep the floor, etc.

This is the way we scrub the clothes, etc.

During the first verse the children skip round in a ring.
They will suggest more actions for themselves.
Use the traditional tune.

Capo 1st fret for chords in brackets

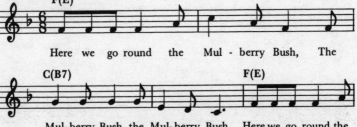

The farmer's in his dell,
The farmer's in his dell,
E . . . I . . . E . . . I
The farmer's in his dell.

The farmer picks a wife, etc.

The wife picks a child, etc.

The child picks a nurse, etc.

The nurse picks a dog, etc.

We all pat the dog, etc.

One child is chosen to be the farmer and stands in a ring formed by the other children. During the first verse the ring moves slowly round the 'farmer' as they sing. During the second verse the 'farmer' chooses a girl to stand with him as a 'wife'. During the third verse the wife chooses someone to be a 'child'. This is repeated with each character until in the last verse all the children pat the 'dog'. Use the traditional tune.

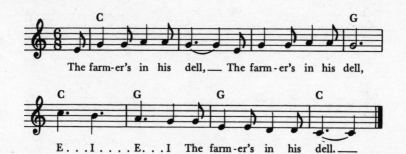

Old MacDonald had a farm,
E–I–E–I–O!
And on that farm he had some cows,
E–I–E–I–O!

With a moo–moo here, and a moo–moo there,
Here a moo, there a moo,
Everywhere a moo–moo!
Old MacDonald had a farm,
E–I–E–I–O!

Each time the verse is sung with a different animal the new noise is added to the chorus, e.g. With a moo–moo here, etc. followed by With a quack–quack here, etc. until all the animal sounds have been included. Very small children may not be able to manage this.

There was a princess long ago,
Long ago, long ago,
There was a princess long ago,
Long ago.

And she lived in a big high tower, etc.

One day a fairy waved her wand, etc.

The princess slept for a hundred years, etc.

A great big forest grew around, etc.

A gallant prince came riding by, etc.

He took his sword and cut it down, etc.

He took her hand to wake her up, etc.

So everybody's happy now, etc.

1st verse: The 'princess' stands in the centre of the ring of children.
2nd verse: The children raise their joined hands to make the tower.
3rd verse: One child, chosen as the fairy, waves her arm over the princess.
4th verse: The princess lies down and closes her eyes.
5th verse: The children wave their arms as trees.
6th verse: One child, chosen as the prince, gallops round the outside of the ring.
7th verse: He pretends to cut down the trees.
8th verse: He wakes up the princess.
9th verse: Children skip round clapping their hands.

There was a prin-cess long a-go,

Long a-go, long a-go, There was a prin-cess

long a-go, Long a - go.

Old Roger is dead and he lies in his grave,
Lies in his grave, lies in his grave.
Old Roger is dead and he lies in his grave,
Heigh-ho, lies in his grave.

Other verses:

They planted an apple tree over his head, etc.

The apples grew ripe and they all tumbled down, etc.

There came an old woman a-picking them up, etc.

Old Roger got up and he gave her a whack, etc.

This made the old woman go hippety-hop, etc.

One child lies in the centre of the ring of children who walk round as they sing.
For apple trees, raise arms above the head.
For apples tumbling, drop fingers with a wriggling movement.
One child then pretends to pick up the apples and put them in her apron.
Roger gets up and whacks her.
The old woman hops all around the ring.

Capo 1st fret for chords in brackets

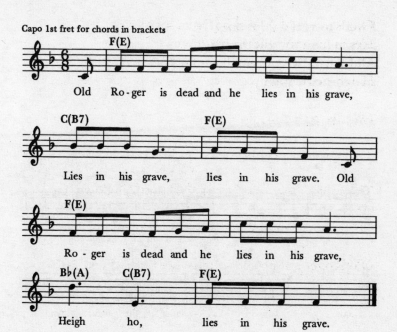

Old Ro-ger is dead and he lies in his grave,

Lies in his grave, lies in his grave. Old

Ro-ger is dead and he lies in his grave,

Heigh ho, lies in his grave.

I went to visit a farm one day:
I saw a (cow) across the way,
And what d'you think I heard it say?
(MOO, MOO, MOO.)

Repeat using different animals.

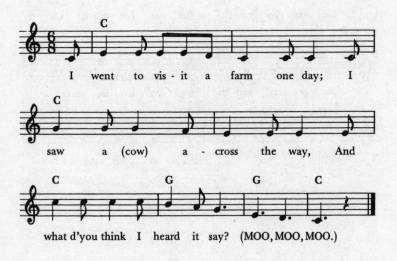

4 Special Occasions

Christmas

Christmas is coming,
We bought a Christmas tree;
We've dressed it up with tinsel,
And with toys for you and me.

Christmas is coming,
I've hung up both my socks;
And when she turned her back I wrapped
Mum's present in a box.

Christmas has come,
The pudding's in the pot;
We're warming up the pudding plates
To make sure it stays hot.

EMM et al.

*This is a variation of Christmas is Coming, the Geese are Getting Fat
and can be sung to the same tune.*

When Santa got stuck up the chimney,
He began to shout;
'You girls and boys won't get any toys
If you don't pull me out!
My beard is black,
There's soot in my sack,
My nose is tickling too.'
When Santa got stuck up the chimney,
ATCHOO! ATCHOO! ATCHOO!

When San-ta got stuck up the chim - ney, He be-gan to shout;— 'You girls and boys won't get a-ny toys If you don't pull me out!'— My beard is black, There's soot in my sack, My nose is tic-kl-ing too'— When San-ta got stuck up the chim-ney, AT-CHOO! AT-CHOO! AT-CHOO!—

Father Christmas, Father Christmas,
He got stuck, he got stuck
Coming down the chimney,
Coming down the chimney,
What bad luck!
What bad luck!

Sung to the tune of I Hear Thunder (see page 53).

Here we go round the Christmas tree,
The Christmas tree, the Christmas tree,
Here we go round the Christmas tree,
On Christmas Day in the morning.

This is the way we put on our scarves, etc.

This is the way we put on our gloves, etc.

This is the way we put on our boots, etc.

ELIZABETH BENNETT

Sung to the tune of Here we go round the Mulberry Bush
(see page 62).

Here we go up to Bethlehem,
Bethlehem, Bethlehem,
Here we go up to Bethlehem,
On Christmas Day in the morning.

Who shall we find in Bethlehem, etc.

The shepherds were there in Bethlehem, etc.

Mary was there in Bethlehem, etc.

Joseph was there in Bethlehem, etc.

Sung to the tune of Here we go round the Mulberry Bush
(see page 62).

The shepherds sat around the fire,
Around the fire, around the fire,
The shepherds sat around the fire,
On a cold winter's night.

The angels came to visit them, etc.
With a bright, shining light.

The wise men travelled from afar, etc.
Following a star.

ZELAH LOCKETT

And so on through the Christmas story.
Older children will make their own
suggestions for other verses.

This is an adaptation of There was a Princess Long Ago
(see page 66).

Children walk round in a circle (for large groups of older children have two rings, one within the other, going in opposite directions) and sing:

Here we go round the Jingle Ring,
The Jingle Ring, the Jingle Ring,
Here we go round the Jingle Ring,
With a hip and a hop and a hie-de-ho!

The children take partners (if there are two rings the child opposite is taken as a partner) and sing:

Take my hand and walk with me,
Walk with me, walk with me,
Take my hand and walk with me,
With a hip and a hop and a hie-de-ho!

as they walk round the ring in pairs. For very young children just one adult would choose one child to walk with her around the outside of the ring while the others stand still and clap hands.
Repeat the circle and circle song then:

Take my hand and skip with me, etc.

Take my hands and swing with me, etc.

Here we go round the Jin - gle Ring, The
Jin - gle Ring, the Jin - gle Ring, Here we go round the
Jin - gle Ring, With a hip and a hop and a hie - de - ho!
Take my hand and walk with me, Walk with me,
walk with me, Take my hand and walk with me, with a
hip and a hop and a hie - de - ho!

We all clap hands together,
We all clap hands together,
We all clap hands together,
When Christmas time is here!

Or Birthday time, Easter time, Holiday time, etc.
(See other suggestions and music on page 188.)

Pull a cracker, pull a cracker,
Till it bangs;
Pull a cracker,
Pull a cracker –
BANG!

A motto and a paper hat
For every one;
Pull a cracker,
Pull a cracker –
BANG!

EMM et al.

Small children can pretend-pull their own cracker.
Older children can pretend with another child.
Give a big clap for the BANG.

Capo 1st fret for chords in brackets

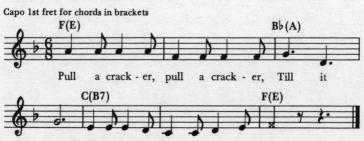

Five mince pies in a baker's shop,
Warm and spicy with sugar on the top;
Along came (Andrew) with a penny one day,
　　Or it could be John, William, Mary, Jane, etc.
He/She bought a mince pie
And ate it right away.

Four mince pies in the baker's shop, etc.

No mince pies left in the baker's shop,
Nothing warm and spicy with sugar on the top;
'Oh dear,' said the baker with the empty tray,
'I'll have to make some more,'
And he did it right away.

So there were
Five mince pies in the baker's shop, etc.

                    SUE BROWNE and ELIZABETH MATTERSON

*This can go on until all the children have had a turn, either one
or more at a time, or as long as anyone wants to carry on singing.
Use the Five Currant Buns tune (see page 51).*

Hurry, little pony, gallop on your way;
For we must be early, don't be late today.

Hurry, hurry, hurry, or we shan't be early,
Hurry, hurry, hurry, or we shan't be early,
Hurry, hurry, hurry, or we shan't be early,
Hurry, little pony, on the way.

    This chorus is repeated after each verse.

Hurry, little pony, on to Bethlehem;
For there is a feast day, two or three of them.

Hurry, little pony, we must find the child;
Born of Mother Mary, Jesus, meek and mild.

ELIZABETH BARNARD

Capo 1st fret for chords in brackets

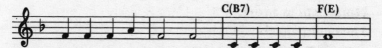

F(E)

Hur-ry, lit-tle po-ny, gal-lop on your way;

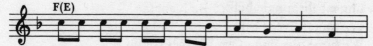

C(B7)　　　　F(E)

For we must be ear-ly, Don't be late to-day.

F(E)

Hur-ry, hur-ry, hur-ry, or we shan't be ear-ly,

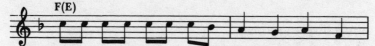

Bb(A)

Hur-ry, hur-ry, hur-ry, or we shan't be ear-ly,

F(E)

Hur-ry, hur-ry, hur-ry, or we shan't be ear-ly,

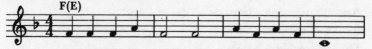

C(B7)　　　　F(E)

Hur-ry, lit-tle po-ny, on the way.

Christmas Eve is here,
And off we go to bed;
As we climb the stairs,
Nodding sleepy heads.
Take our stockings off,
Hang them in a row;
Then jump quickly into bed
And off to sleep we go.

Jingle bells, jingle bells,
Christmas Eve is here;
We hope old Santa Claus comes round
To bring some toys tonight!

Use the tune for Jingle Bells

I'm a little snowman,
Round and fat,
I've got a woolly scarf,
And a little bobble hat;
When the snow is falling
You will hear me say,
'Come and make a snowman on Christmas Day!'

Adaptation of I'm a Little Teapot (see page 52).

Birthdays and Parties

Happy Birthday to you,
Happy Birthday to you,
Happy Birthday, dear (Roger),
Happy Birthday to you!

There are cards and a cake,
There are cards and a cake,
Because it's your Birthday
Happy Birthday to you!

We're having a party, etc.

We'll eat jelly and ice-cream, etc.

There'll be lots of balloons, etc.

We'll play pass the parcel, etc.

EMM et al.

*Ask the children for their suggestions about what
happens at parties.*

For birthdays or as a counting song:

Five little candles
On a Birthday cake;
Let's count them very carefully,
So there's no mistake.

One – Two – Three – Four – Five
    Count on fingers.

We've counted five,
So there's no doubt;
And now it's time
To blow them out.
Fff . . . Fff . . . Fff . . . Fff . . . Fff

Four little candles, etc.

There are none to count,
And there's no doubt;
We're out of puff
Now we've blown them all out.
Fff . . . (*big sigh!*)

Candles on the cake,
Candles on the cake,
(Jonathon) is (three) today
He's going to blow them out.
Huff! Puff! Huff! Puff!
He's going to blow them out.
One (*puff*), two (*puff*), three (*puff*), *etc.*

He's blown the candles out,
He's blown the candles out,
We wish him Happy Birthday,
And Good Luck throughout the year.
Hooray! Hooray! Hooray! . . .
(Or more depending on how many years.)

EMM et al.

Sung to the tune of The Farmer's in his Dell (see page 63).
For one syllable names use Little Anne, or Our friend John,
etc. to fit in the third line.

This Birthday song is used with larger groups and older children:

Birthday candles on a cake,
Standing in a ring;
Light them slowly, one by one,
While the children sing.

Candles on the pretend cake are lit, and the birthday children reply:

I thank you for your greetings,
Your greetings, your greetings;
I thank you for your greetings,
I am (five) years old today.

Other children sing:

Then choose a little playmate,
A playmate, a playmate;
Then choose a little playmate,
To crown you today.

Birthday children choose a friend who crowns them with a birthday crown.

LOVE LANE SCHOOL, ISLE OF WIGHT

Capo 1st fret for chords in brackets

Birth-day can-dles on a cake, Stand-ing in a ring;

Light them slow-ly, one by one, While the child-ren sing.

I thank you for your greet - ings, Your

greet - ings, your greet - ings; I thank you for your

greet - ings, I am 5 years old to - day.

Will you come to my party,
Will you come?
Bring your own cup and saucer,
And a bun;
We'll eat jelly with a spoon,
And play games all afternoon,
Will you come to my party,
Will you come?

EMM et al.

*Ask children what else they do at parties for variations
to the fifth and sixth lines. Rhyming is not important
if the rhythm fits.*

For any kind of party:

There's a party here today, today, today
There's a party here today;
I can tell it by the big balloons,
There's a party here today.

Repeat with different 3rd lines:

I can tell it by the heap of cards,
                    pile of presents,
                    paper hats,
                    bright pink jelly,
                    big iced cake,

and whatever the children like to suggest.

EMM et al.

This is sung to the tune of There is a Tavern in the Town.

The parcel at the party goes round and round,
Round and round, round and round,
The parcel at the party goes round and round,
And now it stops at (Jack)!

The parcel at the party goes round again, etc.

We've taken (one) wrapper from the parcel, etc.

ELIZABETH MATTERSON

Plus any other variations which seem appropriate at the time.
This is sung to the tune of The Wheels on the Bus. (see page 57).

Hallowe'en

Walking out on Hallowe'en,
What did I see?
A little black cat
Purring at me.

Repeat with:

A little brown rat squeaking at me.

A fat yellow pumpkin smiling at me.

BRENDA WEST

*Some children do not like the witch element and it may be best to ask them for their
own suggestions.*

Pumpkin, pumpkin,
Round and fat;
Turn into a Jack-O-Lantern
Just (*clap*)
Like (*clap*)
That! (*clap, clap*)

Easter

The Easter Bunny's feet
Go hop, hop, hop,
Stamp, stamp, stamp.
While his big pink ears
Go flop, flop, flop.
Hands up to head for ears, flopping in turn.
He is rushing on his way
To bring our eggs on Easter Day,
With a hop, flop, hop, flop, hop.
Stamp, flop, stamp, flop, stamp.

*Sing to the tune of Baa, Baa, Black Sheep,
adapted to fit these words.*

Hot Cross Buns,
Hot Cross Buns,
One a penny, two a penny,
Hot Cross Buns.

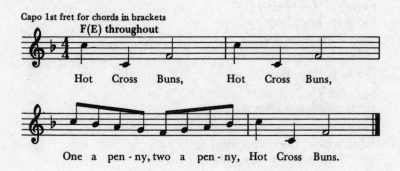

Variations:

Easter Eggs,
Easter Eggs,
We have them at Easter time,
Easter Eggs.

Plus:

Chocolate Rabbits, Chocolate Rabbits, etc.

Simnel Cake, Simnel Cake, etc.

Other things we see at Easter time:

Fluffy yellow chicks,
Fluffy yellow chicks,
We see them at Easter time,
Fluffy yellow chicks.

Woolly little lambs, Woolly little lambs, etc.

EMM et al.

Older children will make their own suggestions.

Variation of Five Currant Buns (see page 51)

Five Hot Cross Buns in a baker's shop,
Round and fat
With a Cross on the top;
Along came (Paul) with just ten p.
He bought a Hot Cross Bun,
And took it home for tea.

Diwali

Diwali is here again,
Diwali is here again,
Shining lanterns,
One, two, three.
Lots of fireworks, lots of noise,
Lots of sweets for girls and boys,
Diwali is here again,
Diwali is here again,
Shining lanterns,
One, two, three!

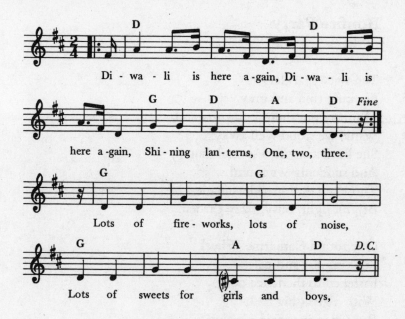

Di - wa - li is here a - gain, Di - wa - li is here a - gain, Shi - ning lan - terns, One, two, three.

Lots of fire - works, lots of noise,

Lots of sweets for girls and boys,

Words and music ELIZABETH BENNETT

Bonfire Party

Ten wiry sparklers
Looking thin and grey,
Mummy put them in the ground,
While we stood well away;
She lit them with a special match,
And suddenly we found
Those ten dull sparklers made a
Bright, light, busy, fizzy garden!

One round Catherine Wheel
Looking flat and pale,
Fastened to the fence post
With a great big nail;
But when the special match
Touched its little paper tail,
It whizzed around quite wildly
In a wheel of coloured sparks!

One huge rocket
Looking rather dull and blue,
Then it went WHOOSH –
And how the sparks flew!
Red and green and gold stars
Falling through the sky,
Ending with a great big BANG!
And then a little sss–igh.

BARNSTAPLE CHILDREN'S LIBRARY
and ELIZABETH MATTERSON

5 *Around the House*

My little house won't stand up straight,
> *Touch fingertips of both hands to make a roof,*
> *rocking from side to side.*

My little house has lost its gate,
> *Drop two little fingers.*

My little house bends up and down,
> *Rock hands violently from side to side.*

My little house is the oldest one in town.
> *Continue rocking hands.*

Here comes the wind; it blows and blows again.
> *Blow through two thumbs.*

Down falls my little house. Oh, what a shame!
> *Drop hands into lap.*

Build a house with five bricks,
One, two, three, four, five.
> *Use clenched fists for bricks, putting one on top of the other five times.*

Put a roof on top
> *Raise both arms above head with fingers touching.*

And a chimney too,
> *Straighten arms.*

Where the wind blows through . . .
WHOO WHOO.
> *Blow hard (or whistle).*

This is the way we wash our clothes,
Rub-a-dub-dub, Rub-a-dub-dub;
See them getting clean and white,
Rub-a-dub, Rub-a-dub-dub!

This is the way we hang them out,
Flippity-flap, Flippity-flap;
See them blowing in the wind,
Flippity-flippity-flap!

This is the way we iron them,
Smooth as can be, smooth as can be;
Soon our wash day will be done,
And nice clean clothes for you and me.

Mime the actions suggested by the words.
Use the tune of Here we go round the Mulberry Bush (see page 62).

Here are the lady's knives and forks,
    Interlace fingers, palms upwards.

Here is the lady's table;
    Turn hands over with fingers still interlaced.

Here is the lady's looking glass,
    Raise two forefingers to a point.

And here is the baby's cradle.
    Raise two little fingers to a point to make
    the other end of the cradle, and rock hands.

I went to the kitchen
And helped Mummy cook,
Helped Mummy cook,
Helped Mummy cook,
I went to the kitchen
And helped Mummy cook,
When she made the dinner.

I went to the garden and helped Daddy there, etc.
When he mowed the lawn.

I went to my Granny's and helped her to sew, etc.
When she made me a dress.

I went with my Grandad and helped him to fish, etc.
When he went to the river.

Children will make suggestions depending on their experience.
Adapt the tune given for I Went to the Garden and Dug up the Ground
(see page 236).

I went to visit a friend one day,
She only lived across the way;
She said she couldn't come out to play
Because it was her washing day.

Followed by:
Ironing day
Polishing day
Baking day
and any other kind of activity the children suggest.

Use the music for I Went to Visit a Farm One Day
(see page 70).

Here is a box;
 Make a box with one fist lightly clenched.

Put on the lid.
 Use the other hand for a lid.

I wonder whatever inside is hid?
 Peep under the lid.

Why, it's a (????) without any doubt.
 Poke one finger through the clenched fist.

Open the box and let it come out!
 Open the fist. Make the appropriate noise for
 whatever object was named.

Suggestions for what is inside the box can include anything
which makes a distinctive noise.

These are Grandmother's glasses,
> *Use thumbs and forefinger to make spectacles.*

This is Grandmother's hat;
> *Both hands flat on head.*

Grandmother claps her hands like this,
> *Little double clap.*

And folds them in her lap.
> *Lay hands overlapping in lap.*

These are Grandfather's glasses,
> *As above.*

This is Grandfather's hat;
> *Use one hand to make a peak over eyes.*

This is the way he folds his arms,
> *Fold arms from elbow.*

And has a little nap. Zzzzzz!
> *Close eyes, give a little snore.*

My dolly has to stay in bed,
Tucked up warm and tight;
She has some pains in her poor head,
And spots came out last night.
The doctor came and saw her chest,
It was red as red could be;
He told me what I should have guessed,
She's got (measles),
Just like me!

Or chicken pox, nettle rash or whatever the children suggest.
This can be sung to the first part of the tune for Between the
Valley and the Hill (see page 243).

Three little monkeys were jumping on the bed,
One fell off and bumped his head;
His mummy called the doctor
And the doctor said,
'No more jumping on the bed!'

Two little monkeys were jumping on the bed,
One fell off and bumped his head;
His mummy called the doctor
And the doctor said,
'Do keep those monkeys off that bed!'

One little monkey was jumping on the bed,
He fell off and bumped his head;
His mummy called the doctor
And the doctor said,
'Well, that's what you get for jumping on the bed!'

There were ten in the bed,
And the little one said,
'Roll over! Roll over!'
So they all rolled over
And one fell out.
He gave a little scream – 'OW!'
He gave a little shout – 'HEY!
That was very mean!'

So there were
Nine in the bed, etc.

So there was one in the bed,
He turned over and said,
'Lucky me! Lucky me!
Now they've all rolled over
There's more room for me . . .
Its much nicer in bed
With no one sitting on your head.
Now I can go to sleep! . . . Aaaaahhh' (*big sigh*)

EMM et al.

*For small children it may be better to start with five
in the bed.*

Capo 1st fret for chords in brackets
F(E) throughout

There were ten in the bed, And the lit-tle one said 'Roll

ov-er! Roll ov-er!' So they all rolled ov-er And

one fell out. He gave a lit-tle scream OW! He

gave a lit-tle shout HEY! That was ve-ry mean. So there were

The baby in the cradle
Goes rock–a–rock–a–rock,
> *Fold arms and rock them.*

The clock on the dresser
Goes tick–a–tick–a–tock;
> *One forefinger wags from side to side like a pendulum.*

The rain on the window
Goes tap–a–tap–a–tap,
> *Tap with fingers on table or floor.*

But here comes the sun,
So we clap–a–clap–a–clap!
> *Clap to words.*

In my house there is a room,
And in that room there is a bed,
And in that bed there's a little Teddy Bear
With a very bad cold in his head, Atchoo!
With a very bad cold in his head.

*This can be sung to the tune of Jack and Jill went up the Hill
if the rhythm is slightly adapted to fit these words and the last
line is repeated.*

I know a house, it's a cold old house,
A cold old house by the sea . . . Brrrrr;
> *Big shiver.*

If I were a mouse in that cold old house,
What a cold, cold mouse I would be . . . Brrrrr!
> *Big shiver and curl up small.*

Mousie, Mousie, where's your house?
Underneath the floor,
Behind the kitchen door,
Is that your house?

Mousie, Mousie, are you in?
Can you hear me calling?
Can you hear me calling?
Just say Squeak! Squeak!
If you're in.

Mousie, Mousie, are you coming out to play?
The cat's away,
So it's safe today –
It's quite safe to
Come and play.

Mousie, Mousie, the cat's come home,
It's not safe to roam,
While the cat's at home,
So please stay safe
In your house.

DIANA LOWE and ELIZABETH MATTERSON

Creep, Mousie, creep,
Creep, Mousie, creep;
The old cat lies asleep,
The old cat lies asleep;
But take care when her whiskers twitch,
Very great care when her whiskers twitch;
And keep quite still,
Stay very STILL!

Sung to the tune for Three Blind Mice. One child is the sleeping cat and the others creep round her. On the last 'STILL' they must freeze . . . and the cat can claim anyone she sees move to stay with her in the ring, until there is only one mouse left and he becomes the cat. To speed things up for very small children the first mouse to be caught becomes the cat so that they all get a turn more quickly.

In a cottage in a wood,
> *Make a roof shape with hands.*

A little old man at the window stood;
> *Look through thumbs and forefingers.*

He saw a rabbit running by
> *Pound feet on the floor.*

Who knocked on his front door.
> *Knock one fist on the other open hand.*

'Help me! Help me!' the rabbit cried,
> *Hands held up in fright . . . and say this part.*

'Or the hunter will shoot me dead!'
> *Pretend to aim and shoot.*

'Little rabbit, come inside –
> *Beckon with forefinger . . . and use last two lines of the tune.*

And be safe with me instead.'
> *Fold arms.*

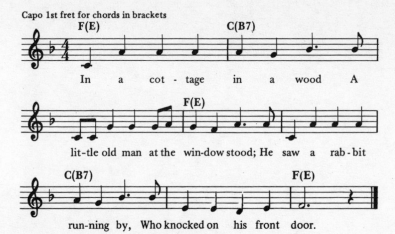

6 Things We Like to Eat

Chop, chop, choppity-chop,
Cut off the bottom
And cut off the top;
What there is left we will
Put in the pot;
Chop, chop, choppity-chop.

(*Sniff*) Mmm (*Sniff*) Mmm . . . Lovely!

This is chanted rather than sung.
Children suggest vegetables for soup and 'cry'
when peeling the onions, scrape the carrots,
chop really hard for swedes. The suggestions may
get wilder e.g. put ME in the pot, which adds
to the game.

Slice, slice, the bread looks nice,
Spread, spread, butter on the bread;
On the top we'll put some (jam),
Now it's even nicer for us to eat!

Repeat with all the other suggestions the children make
for what they like on their bread.

Five cherry cakes in a baker's shop,
Adult holds up five fingers.

Round and fat with icing on the top;

*Stop at this point and ask the chosen child how many
he wants to buy for his family.*

Along came (Luke) with (three) 10ps,
He bought (three) cherry cakes
Adult puts down one, two, three fingers.

And took them home for tea.

So . . . how many are left in the shop?
Count fingers still left up.

There were one . . . two . . . left in the shop!

*Ask the children for more suggestions, then depending on whatever they choose
e.g. doughnuts, jam tarts, buttered scones:*

Five brown biscuits in a baker's shop,
Crunchy and munchy with chocolate on the top, etc.

Use the tune for Five Currant Buns (see page 51)

*Older children may start using their own fingers to count or five children can be
used as cakes and counted.*

   *This can also be developed as a memory game for one child or a group of
children using coloured counters to represent cakes and working out what the baker
has left in his shop after several different purchases have been made.*

Old Tom Tomato, like a red ball,
Basked in the sunshine by the garden wall.
  Make fist into a ball.

Along came Benjamin with his mouth open wide
And old Tom Tomato popped inside.
  Open mouth and put fingers in.

Down, down, down, down the red lane –
  Stroke throat.

We won't see old Tom Tomato again.
But Benjamin chuckled and said, 'Ha ha!
I like red tomatoes, please give me some more.'
  Hold out hand.

Jelly on the plate,
Jelly on the plate;
Wibble-wobble,
Wibble-wobble,
Jelly on the plate!

Followed by:
Yellow jelly on the plate,
Red and yellow jelly on the plate,
Green, red and yellow jelly on the plate, etc.

This is really a skipping song but small children are happy to wibble-wobble their arms and legs while sitting on a chair. Adding the colours is quite difficult and very small children may not manage more than Yellow jelly.

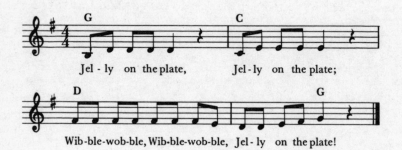

Jel - ly on the plate,   Jel - ly on the plate;

Wib-ble-wob-ble, Wib-ble-wob-ble, Jel - ly on the plate!

I had a little cherry stone
And put it in the ground,

> *Pretend to put cherry in left hand using right thumb and forefinger.*

And when next year I went to look,
A tiny shoot I found.

> *Right forefinger 'grows' up from clenched left fist.*

The shoot grew upwards day by day,

> *Both hands rise upwards.*

And soon became a tree.
I picked the rosy cherries then,

> *Right hand stays up as tree, and left hand picks cherries.*

And ate them for my tea.

BOYCE and BARTLETT

This can be sung to the tune of I had a Little Nut Tree.

Mix a pancake,
Stir a pancake,
Pop it in the pan;
Fry a pancake,
Toss a pancake,
Catch it if you can!

CHRISTINA ROSSETTI

This can be sung to the tune of One potato, Two potato.

Roly–poly pudding and blackberry pie,

Roll fists, indicate shape of pie with forefingers.

Peter likes the pudding, and Polly likes the pie;

One thumb up for Peter, other for Polly.

Which one do you like? Oh my! my!

Point to friend, rub tummy.

I like roly–poly pudding

And blackberry pie!

As first line.

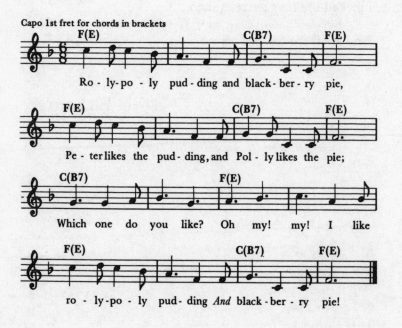

Capo 1st fret for chords in brackets

Mummy made pancakes on Tuesday,
She tossed them in the air,
One fell on the table,
One fell on the chair;
One fell on the cooker,
One fell on the grate;
But, luckily for me,
I had three
Because they fell on my plate!

SHAUN FOUNTAIN

We're going to make a cake, we're going to make a
    cake;
We're going to make it really big,
       Indicate how big with hands.
Because we all like cake.

Ask children what to put in it.

Raisins in the bowl, raisins in the bowl;
Stir it with a great big spoon,
       Stir vigorously.
Raisins in the bowl.

Currants, cherries, etc. follow.

Put it in the oven, put it in the oven;
Take care not to slam the door,
       Loud CLAP.
Until it's nicely cooked.

Icing on the top, etc.
Spread it with a big, flat knife,
       Spread carefully.
Icing on the top.

We all have a piece, etc.
Some for you and some for me,
       Point to neighbour and to self.
There's some for everyone.
       Everybody eats their cake.

And now it's all . . . gone!
       Say this line slowly.

EMM et al.

Sing to the tune of The Farmer's in his Dell (see page 63).
This can also be used as an activity game where different children come to stir in
the ingredient of their choice, spread the icing, cut the cake, hand it round.

One potato, two potato,
Three potato, four;
I like mashed potato,
May I have some more?
Pleeeease!

For other verses, consult the children.
I like crispy chips, etc.
I like potato crisps, etc.
I like roast potatoes, etc.

I like potato cakes, etc.
I like new potatoes, etc.
I like jacket potatoes, etc.

EMM et al.

*Use the familiar tune for One potato, Two potato, and say the Pleeeease very slowly.
This song can also be used for different foods, e.g. One banana, Two banana, or
One ripe mango, Two ripe mangoes.*

I've got a basket of apples,
Indicate basket with arms.

Picked from a tree,
Reach up high to pick apples.

Apples rosy-red for you,
Point to friend.

And shiny green for me;
Point to self.

Some of them are big,
Some of them are small,
Hands cupped wide, hands cupped small.

Some of them are oval,
Some are like a ball;
Indicate shapes with forefingers.

Some of them are sour . . .ugh!
Pull a face.

Some of them are sweet . . .mmn,
Big wide smile.

Lots of lovely apples
For you and me to eat.
Fist on fist to indicate a pile.

EMM et al.

Sing to the tune of Christmas is Coming, the Geese are Getting Fat, adapted to fit the rhythm of the words.

Bread and jam,
Bread and jam,
I like it,
> *Point to self.*

Do you like it?
> *Point to friend.*

We both like bread and jam!
> *Nod vigorously.*

Fish and chips, fish and chips, etc.

Eggs and bacon, eggs and bacon, etc.

EMM et al.

And whatever else the children like to choose.
Use the tune for Hot Cross Buns (see page 94).

Eggs and bacon,
Eggs and bacon;
Scrambled eggs,
Scrambled eggs;
Sausage and tomato,
Sausage and tomato;
Beans on toast,
Beans on toast.

EMM et al.

Sing to the tune I Hear Thunder (see page 53).
Older children may be able to make up their own version when they get a feeling
for the rhythm needed.
It can also be used as an 'echo' song where the adult (or half the group) sings the
first half of each phrase and the children (or other half of the group) repeat it.

Curry and rice,
Curry and rice,
Everybody here likes
Curry and rice.
We eat it all day,
Never throw it away;
We all like
Curry and rice.

Other suggestions: Mango ice-cream, Roti and dahl,
Sausage and chips, depending on what the children suggest.

Words and music ELIZABETH BENNETT

Chapatti in your hand,
Chapatti in your hand;
Clap it here,
Clap it there,
Chapatti in your hand!

Spaghetti on your fork,
Spaghetti on your fork;
Twirl it round
And twirl it round,
Spaghetti on your fork!

Prawn balls in your chopsticks,
Prawn balls in your chopsticks;
Hold them tight,
Don't let them slip,
Prawn balls in your chopsticks!

Followed by anything else the children think of which can be
fitted to the rhythm, e.g. Soup in a bowl, Sandwich in your fingers,
Sausages on sticks, etc.

ELIZABETH BENNETT

This is sung to the tune of Jelly on the Plate (see page 118).

I like bananas, monkey nuts and grapes.
That's why they call me
Tarzan of the Apes!

Oh, Mum, will you buy me,
Please buy me, please buy me,
Oh, Mum, will you buy me,
Buy me a banana?

Oh, Mum, would you like a bite,
A little bite, just a LITTLE bite,
Oh, Mum, would you like a bite,
A bite of my banana?

Followed by:

Oh, Dad, would you like a bite, etc.
Oh, Grannie, would you like a bite, etc.
Oh, Auntie, would you like a bite, etc.

Oh, Mum, now it's all gone,
It's all gone, IT'S ALL GONE!
Oh, Mum, will you buy me,
Another banana?

This is a version of an old street song from Belfast and can be sung to an adaptation
of There's a Hole in my Bucket, the tune also used for There's a Fly on my Ice-
cream (see page 133). The people being offered bites can be children in the group
instead of family members.

A peanut lay on the railway track,
Its heart was all a-flutter;
Along came a train and squashed it flat,
And made it into peanut butter.

The driver climbed down with some bread,
And he was heard to mutter,
'It's a shame to leave it on the track . . .
I quite like peanut butter!'

Second verse ELIZABETH MATTERSON

This can be sung to the tune of Polly Wolly Doodle.

Hippety Hop to the corner shop,
To buy some sweeties for Sunday;
Some for you,
Some for me,
And some for sister Sandy.

Followed by:

The baker's shop to buy some bread for Monday
The butcher's shop to buy some meat for Tuesday
The fishmonger's shop to buy some kippers for
   Wednesday
The grocer's shop to buy some sugar for Thursday
The dairy shop to buy some butter for Friday
The greengrocer's shop to buy some apples for Saturday

EMM et al.

*Older children will make their own suggestions as to which shop and what to buy.
Another variation is to use the same shop (a supermarket if that is all very young
children would be familiar with) for each day but to buy something different that
would be sold there.*

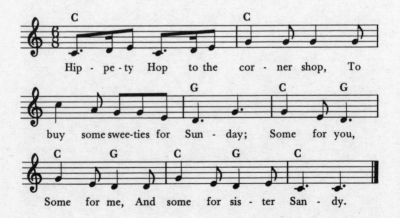

Old MacDonald had a shop,
E–I–E–I–O;
And in that shop he had some burgers,
E–I–E–I–O;
With a Big Mac here,
And a French Fries there,
Here a Coke, there a Coke,
Everywhere a Coke, Coke,
Old MacDonald had a shop,
E–I–E–I–O!

This version of Old MacDonald will depend on the children's experience. Those who are familiar with other take-away chains may well suggest other variations and make up their own tunes.

Yellow butter, purple jelly, red jam, black bread.
Spread it thick,
Say it quick,
Yellow butter, purple jelly, red jam, black bread.
Spread it thicker,
Say it quicker,
Yellow butter, purple jelly, red jam, black bread.
Now repeat it,
While you eat it,
Yellow butter, purple jelly, red jam, black bread . . .
Don't talk
With your mouth full!

MARY ANN HOBERMAN

*Very small children may only get as far as the first
four lines.*

Nobody loves me,
Everybody hates me,
I think I'll go and eat worms;
Big fat juicy ones,
Long thin wiggly ones,
See how they wriggle and they squirm.

*This can be sung to the tune of Polly Wolly Doodle.
Not every group of children would like this but those
who do appear to enjoy it enormously.*

'Georgie' sings: There's a fly on my ice-cream,
Dear Mummy, dear Mummy,
There's a fly on my ice-cream,
Dear Mummy, a fly!

'Mummy' replies: Give it to me then, dear Georgie,
Dear Georgie, dear Georgie,
Give it to me then, dear Georgie,
Dear Georgie, give it to me!

'Georgie' sings: I can't give it to you, dear Mummy, etc.
Dear Mummy, I can't!

'Mummy' asks: Why can't you, dear Georgie, etc.
Just give it to me!

'Georgie' wails: Because I've swallowed it, dear
Mummy, etc.
I've swallowed it . . . Ugh!

Followed by: Caterpillar on my lettuce,
Sand in my sandwich,
Grub in my apple.

EMM et al.

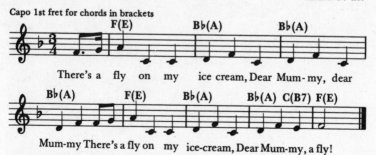

Capo 1st fret for chords in brackets

There's a fly on my ice cream, Dear Mum-my, dear
Mum-my There's a fly on my ice-cream, Dear Mum-my, a fly!

Pussy cat, Pussy cat,
Where have you been?
Licking your lips
With your whiskers so clean.
Pussy cat, Pussy cat,
Purring and Pudgy,
Pussy cat, Pussy cat,
Where is our BUDGIE?

MAX FATCHEN

Little Mary, looking wistful,
Eats her jelly by the fistful;
On the floor it slips and sloshes,
That's why everyone
Wears galoshes!

MAX FATCHEN

Sing to the tune of Bobby Shafto.

Wet Weather

Pitter, patter, pit, pat,
Listen to the rain
Falling in the garden,
And down the window pane.

Pitter, patter, pit, pat,
Where can be the sun?
Do you think he's hiding,
Hiding just for fun?

Pitter, patter, pit, pat
It was just a shower
Washing all the green leaves,
Sprinkling every flower.

Paddling in the puddles,
Paddling in the puddles,
Paddling in the puddles,
But don't let Mummy see!

When the rain comes falling down,
Cleaning up the dirty town,
Filling all the gutters full,
As the children go to school.

Paddling in the puddles, etc.

Pad-dling in   the pud-dles,   Pad-dling in   the pud-dles,

Pad-dling in   the pud-dles,   But don't let Mum-my   see!

When the rain comes fal-ling down, clean-ing up the   dir - ty town,

Fil-ling all the   gut-ters full,   As the child-ren go to school.

'Splash,' said a raindrop
As it fell upon my hat;
'Splash,' said another
As it trickled down my back.
'You are very rude,' I said
As I looked up to the sky;
Then ANOTHER raindrop splashed
Right into my eye!

Walking through the raindrops,
What did I see?
A wet little puppy dog
Coming towards me.

Variations:

Walking through the sunshine, etc. a hot little puppy
   dog . . .

Walking through the snowflakes, etc. a white little
   puppy dog . . .

Walking down the windy street, etc. a ruffled little
   puppy dog . . .

Walking through the shadows, etc. a dark little puppy
   dog . . .

                       EMM et al.

Children will suggest their own versions,
This can be sung to a simple version of the tune for
The Grand Old Duke of York if the rhythm is adjusted.

Cold Weather

The North Wind doth blow,
And we shall have snow,
And what will the robin do then,
Poor thing?
He'll sleep in the barn,
To keep himself warm,
And hide his head under his wing,
Poor thing!

The North Wind doth blow,
And we shall have snow,
And what will the children do then,
Poor things?
When lessons are done,
They will skip, hop and run,
To keep warm till Spring comes again,
Poor things!

Capo 1st fret for chords in brackets

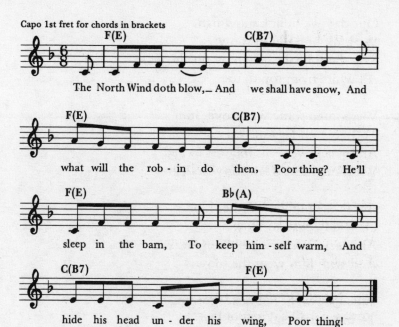

The North Wind doth blow,— And we shall have snow, And what will the rob-in do then, Poor thing? He'll sleep in the barn, To keep him-self warm, And hide his head un-der his wing, Poor thing!

One day we built a snowman,
We built him out of snow;
You should have seen how fine he was,
All white from top to toe.

We poured some water over him,
To freeze his legs and ears;
And when we went indoors to bed,
We thought he'd last for years.

But in the night a warmer kind
Of wind began to blow;
And Jack Frost cried and ran away,
And with him went the snow.

When we went out next morning
To bid our friend 'Good Day',
There wasn't any snowman there . . .
He'd melted right away!

This fits the tune of My Old Man's a Dustman.

There were five little snowmen,
Each with scarf and woolly hat,
Out came the sun
And
      melted
              one;
It's sad –
But that was that!

There were four little snowmen, etc.

There are no little snowmen,
Just scarves and woolly hats,
Sitting in a puddle
In a
      very wet
              muddle;
It's sad –
But that is that!

EMM et al.

Use the tune for There were Five Little Spacemen
(see page 295).

Who made the footprints in the snow?
Who came along?
And where did they go?

The farmer's wife has just been out
To scatter bits of bread about;
So she made footprints in the snow . . .

A little sparrow was out today,
He ate some bread, then hopped away;
So he made footprints in the snow . . .

A rabbit hurried on his way,
It's too cold outside for him today;
So he made footprints in the snow . . .

A duck went off to have a swim,
The pond was not too cold for him;
So he made footprints in the snow . . .

I went out across the way,
To ask my friend to come and play;
So I made footprints in the snow.

TOM STANIER/BBC TV

A chubby little snowman
Had a carrot nose;
Along came a rabbit
And what do you suppose?
That hungry little bunny,
Looking for his lunch,
ATE the snowman's carrot nose . . .
Nibble, nibble, CRUNCH!

Sing to the tune of I had a Little Nut Tree.

Here we go round the Mulberry Bush,
The Mulberry Bush, the Mulberry Bush;
Here we go round the Mulberry Bush,
On a cold and frosty morning.

We stamp our feet to keep them warm,
Stamp our feet to keep them warm;
We stamp our feet to keep them warm,
On a cold and frosty morning.

Followed by:
We clap our hands to keep them warm, etc.

We jump about to keep everything warm, etc.

and anything else the children suggest.
Sing to the tune of Here we go round the Mulberry Bush
(see page 62)

Sunshine

(Sally) go round the sun,
Sally go round the moon;
Sally go round the chimney pots
On a (Sunday) afternoon.

*If the group has enough staying power, go through the days of the week with
different children and finish with:*

We all went round the sun,
We all went round the moon;
We all went round the chimney pots
On a Sunday, Monday, Tuesday, Wednesday, Thursday,
    Friday, Saturday
And again . . . on Sunday afternoon!

Last verse ELIZABETH MATTERSON

*This is an old ring game. A useful version for small
children is to choose one child for the sun and another
for the moon. They sit in the middle of the ring made by
the other sitting children. (Sally), or whichever named
child, goes round the sun, then round the moon, then in and
out the other children until she gets back to her
place. This is repeated with another named child for
Monday, Tuesday, etc. Small children or those who need help
can be taken round by an adult.*

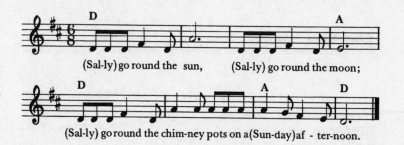

(Sal-ly) go round the sun,   (Sal-ly) go round the moon;

(Sal-ly) go round the chim-ney pots on a (Sun-day) af - ter-noon.

Day and Night

Mr Moon, you're up too soon,
The sun's still in the sky;
Go back to bed
And cover your head,
You must wait till the day's gone by.

This can be sung to a simple version of the tune for
Jack and Jill went up the Hill.

Twinkle, twinkle, little star,
How I wonder what you are;
Up above the world so high
Like a diamond in the sky;
Twinkle, twinkle, little star
How I wonder what you are.

When the blazing sun is gone,
When he nothing shines upon;
Then you show your little light
Twinkle, twinkle, through the night.
Twinkle, twinkle, little star, etc.

Use the traditional tune.

Five small stars that shone so bright,
Hold up five fingers and wriggle them.
Were dancing about in the sky one night;
A cloud came slowly drifting by,
Clasp hands high above head and move arms gently.
Then only four stars shone in the sky.
Hold up four fingers.

Four small stars, etc. *till there are none.*

No small stars were shining bright,
No little stars to dance in the night;
But the cloud moved on, and by and by
Those five small stars shone again in the sky.

MADGE BUGDEN and ELIZABETH MATTERSON

In a dark little town
There was a dark little house;
In the dark little house
There was a dark little room;
In the dark little room
There was a warm little bed,
And in the warm little bed
There was (William).

But in the morning when the sun came up . . .

It woke up the dark little town,
It woke up the dark little house,
It woke up the dark little room,
It made everything light and bright;
And in the warm little bed,
(William) sat up and said,
'Good morning!'

EMM et al.

8 *Songs for Groups*

Hello and Goodbye

Hello Peter, hello Adam,
Hello Anne,
Hello Helen;
Hello Ruth and David,
Hello William and Katy,
We're glad you're here,
We're glad you're here!

Use the Frère Jacques tune.
This can also be used for marking a register, e.g.

Where is Peter?, Where is Adam?
  Each child acknowledges his name.
Where is Anne? etc.
Are they here?
Yes, they're here!

Goodbye (Peter), goodbye (Anne),
Goodbye (William),
It's time we all went home!

Repeat until all the children have had their goodbye.
This can be speeded up if necessary by saying three names
at a time on the same note or with:

Goodbye girls, goodbye boys,
Goodbye children,
It's time we all went home!

EMM et al.

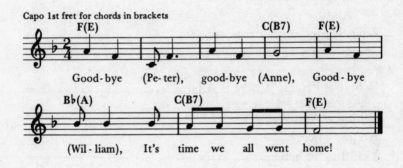

What We Do

What do we do when we go to (nursery)?
What do we do when we go to (nursery)?
What do we do when we go to (nursery)?
When we go to play!

We make sand-pies in the sand-pit, etc.
When we go to play!

We paint pictures at the easel, etc.

We stick boxes with some glue, etc.

We pour water at the tray, etc.

We climb the frame out in the garden, etc.

EMM et al.

Ask the children for suggestions.
Sing to the tune of What shall we do with the Drunken Sailor.
This is a simple but very adaptable song. It works equally well for going to
Grannie's, Auntie's, the shops, the library (we choose books with lots of pictures),
on holiday (we go to the seaside on the train), on picnics (we eat sandwiches and
apples).

We (Johnnie) went to the (nursery)
And played with the (sand),
Played with the sand,
Played with the sand;
We went to the nursery,
And played with the sand
And now we're (he's) going home.

We'll (He'll) come back tomorrow (on Monday)
And play with the (bricks)
Play with the bricks
Play with the bricks
We'll come back tomorrow
And play with the bricks
We'll be back in the morning (on Monday morning).

EMM et al.

*This is sung to the tune of Old Roger is Dead
(see page 69).
This is particularly useful for new children to give
them the idea of continuity, and that there is
something nice to look forward to the next time they
go to their group.*

What did (Mary) do today?
What did (Mary) do today?
She painted a picture and put it to dry.

Or
Played with the dollies and put them to bed
Built with the bricks and made a big tower
Played with the sand and made a sand-castle
Rode on the bike till his legs were tired
Played with the glue and stuck boxes together

depending on what the children did.
This is sung to the first part of the tune of Wind the Bobbin Up
(see page 61).
This song can be used at home and is also particularly useful
in the group as a reminder for both children and adults as to what
each child did.

Wash your dirty hands,
Wash your dirty hands;
Rub and scrub,
Rub and scrub,
Wash your dirty hands.

Wipe the sticky table,
Wipe the sticky table;
Wipe it clean
And wipe it dry,
Wipe the sticky table.

*This is sung to the tune of The Farmer's in his Dell (see page 63)
and can be adapted for any activity from teeth-cleaning,
folding clothes, packing away toys, closing doors and
locking gates to saying goodbye at the end of a session.*

We're all going home,
We're all going home,
Goodbye to (Peter),
Goodbye to (Jane),
Goodbye to everyone.

Who Are You, Who Am I?

Edward Whitham, Edward Whitham,
Where are you?
There he is, there he is;
How do you do!

This variation of Tommy Thumb (see page 48), is used for
different children by changing the name and for different
situations by changing the last line, e.g.
Milk time: It's milk time for you.
Giving out Christmas presents: Happy Christmas to you.
Going home time: Here's your painting.

Mother's washing, Mother's washing,
Rub, rub, rub;
Picked up (Johnny)'s little shirt
And threw it in the tub!

Mother's outside, Mother's outside,
Hanging clothes up high;
Pegging out (Deborah)'s stripy dress
To let it get quite dry!

Mother's ironing, Mother's ironing,
Press and press away
Ironing (Timmy)'s bright red trousers
So he'll look smart today!

Mother's finished, Mother's finished
Hip hooray!
Johnny's little shirt . . .
Deborah's stripy dress . . .
Timmy's bright red trousers, etc.
Are clean to wear today!

ELIZABETH BARNARD (1st verse)
EMM et al. (other verses)

Each child who has been featured in the song stands up in turn to help everyone to remember the list at the end.

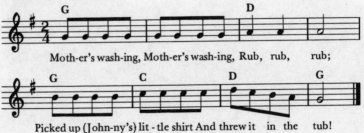

Moth-er's wash-ing, Moth-er's wash-ing, Rub, rub, rub;

Picked up (John-ny's) lit-tle shirt And threw it in the tub!

Emma and Jo are in the ring,
Tra la la la la;
Emma and Jo are in the ring,
Tra la la la la la;
Emma and Jo are in the ring,
Tra la la la la;
And now they change with
(Tim and Mark).

*Each of the two children choose someone to change
places with them and the song changes to use the names
of the new children.
Use the tune for Brown Girl in the Ring.*

These variations of The Bear Walked over the Mountain (see page 178) give an opportunity for all the children's names to be used.

The crocodile swam in the river, etc.
To see what there was for his tea.

But all that he could see,
But all that he could see,
Was Billy and Philip and Rachel,
Mandy and Julie and Nigel,
Polly and Susan and Richard . . .
And he ate them for his tea!

The 'crocodile' walks round the outside of the ring of children until the point in the song to make his choice of children to eat.
The last child is the next one to walk round the ring.

The bee buzzed round the bushes . . .
To see who he could sting, etc.
Were all he tried to sting.

The spider climbed up the curtain, etc.
Were all he managed to tickle.

EMM et al.

Where is Thomas?
Sitting next to David;
Where is David?
Sitting next to Anne.

Where is Anne?
etc.

EMM et al.

*This can go all round the ring. If there is a large
number of children and it would take too long,
miss out the second reference to David and go
straight on to Anne and her neighbour.*

This old man, he played one,
He dropped a hammer on (Philip's) thumb;
With a nick-nack, paddy-whack,
Give the dog a bone,
This old man came rolling home!

One: He dropped a hammer on (Philip's) thumb.
Two: He took the buckle from (Mary's) shoe.
Three: He threw a ball at (Andrew's) knee.
Four: He rang the bell on (Rebecca's) door.
Five: He chased (Daniel) round a beehive.
Six: He whacked (Deborah) with some sticks.
Seven: He followed (Sarah) down to Devon.
Eight: He knocked hard on (Matthew's) gate.
Nine: He saw (Thomas) near the railway line.
Ten: He took (Susan's) big fat hen.

*The named child comes to stand by the adult each time
while 'his' verse is sung.*

If you're (Rosie) and you know it
Clap your hands;
If you're Rosie and you know it
Clap your hands;
If you want *us* all to know it
Then you'll really have to show it,
If you're Rosie and you know it,
Clap your hands.

*This is a 'personalized' version of If you're Happy and
you Know it (see page 186). Other named children can be
asked to stamp feet, shake heads, stand up straight, walk
round the chair, pull a face, etc. to identify themselves.*

My friend (Sarah) walks like this,
Walks like this,
Walks like this;
My friend Sarah walks like this
On her way to school.

*Other named friends hop, skip, run, dance to other
destinations*, e.g.

My friend (Daniel) pedals his bike like this, etc.
On his way to the shops.

*Sing to the tune of Heads and Shoulders (see page 191),
slightly adapted for the last line.*

(Mary) wore her red dress,
Red dress, red dress;
Mary wore her red dress
All day long.

*Change the name for different children and mention
what they are wearing.*

Capo 1st fret for chords in brackets

Ten (Five) green bottles
Hanging on a wall;
Ten green bottles hanging on a wall,
If (Johnny) (Polly, Ruth and Sarah) should knock a
  bottle
So that it accidentally falls,
There'll be (nine) green bottles
Hanging on the wall.

This old favourite is very adaptable and can be used to
include several children, using the same note to
sing their names. The number of bottles left will
depend on the number of names included. Another version
has some of the children representing the bottles so
that the number left each time can be counted ready to
start the next verse. Very young children would not
manage to count down from ten and starting with five
would be better for them.

(Patrick) was a postman,
A postman, a postman;
Patrick was a postman
All day long.

He posted all the letters,
The letters, the letters;
He posted all the letters
Yes that is what he did.

Each child chooses what he wants to be and tells
(and shows) everyone what that person does.
This is sung to the tune for Mary Wore her Red Dress
(see page 166).

John Brown met a little Indian,
John Brown met a little Indian,
John Brown met a little Indian,
One little Indian boy.

Chorus:
He met one little, two little, three little Indians,
Four little, five little, six little Indians,
Seven little, eight little, nine little Indians,
Ten little Indian boys.

John Brown met two little Indians, etc.

This game can be played with fingers, in which case the last verse is at ten little Indians.
If it is played as a 'bringing in' game it can go on until all the children have been brought into the group.

Variations:

This is an excellent counting song in its own right, but the melody, style and rhythm also make it a useful basis for alternative songs and variations (see pages 189, 195, 266), for improvisations to suit any situation or theme, and for including all the children in a group, e.g.

Peter Gray would like (had) a bicycle for Christmas
(his Birthday), etc.
With two pedals (handlebars) and a bell!

Utah is our Japanese friend,
Our Japanese friend, our Japanese friend,
Utah is our Japanese friend,
He meets us at the nursery!

Chorus:
He knows Mary and David and Peter and Susan, etc.
Who all come to the nursery!

(Utah shakes hands with/bows to/hugs each friend)

Capo 1st fret for chords in brackets

John Brown met a lit-tle In-dian, John Brown
met a lit-tle In - dian, John Brown
met a lit - tle In - dian, One lit - tle In - dian
boy. He met one lit - tle, two lit - tle,
three lit - tle In - dians, Four lit - tle, five lit - tle,
six lit - tle In - dians, Seven lit - tle, eight lit - tle,
nine lit - tle In - dians, Ten lit - tle In - dian boys.

(This old American folk song is usually associated with the John Brown who was involved with the freeing of American slaves. The Indians referred to were native American Indians. The full version of the song had succeeding verses: Each little Indian had a bow and arrow/little tepee/tomahawk/feather head–dress/totem–pole, etc.)

Using Musical Instruments

It's the music box,
It's the music box,
What shall we play today?
We will play the (drums).
>   *3 beats on (drum).*
We will play the drums.
>   *3 beats on drum.*
That's what we'll play today!

*Practise this just clapping or tapping, then introduce
instruments gradually.*

Variation:

How shall we play today, etc. *to introduce* loudly, quietly,
fast, slowly, etc.

Capo 1st fret for chords in brackets

It's the mu - sic box, It's the mu - sic box,

What shall we play to - day? We will play the drums.

1, 2, 3! We will play the drums. 1, 2, 3!

That's what we'll play to - day.

Words and music SUE WHITHAM

Tambourine, tambourine,
How do you play?
Tap, tap, tap,
     Tap tambourine.
Tap, tap, tap,
All through the day.

*Practise this first just clapping or pretending to use
instruments on 'Tap, tap, tap', until the children get the
idea that the instruments are only played at the
appropriate points in the song.*

Follow with:
Little drums, Little drums, etc. Bom-bom-bom, Bom-
    bom-bom, etc.
then other instruments, e.g. Triangle . . . Ting-ting-ting.
Then:
Orchestra, orchestra, . . .
Quietly, quietly, All through the day.
Loudly, loudly, All through the day.

Words and music DOT PHILLIPS

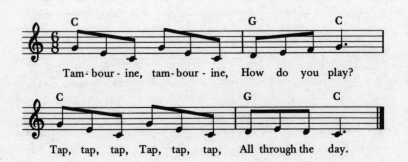

Oh, we can play on the big bass drum,
And this is the music to it;
Boom, boom, boom goes the big bass drum,
And that's the way we do it.

Oh, we can play on the triangle, etc.
(Ting, ting, ting)

Oh, we can play on the castanets, etc.
(Clack, clack, clack)

The children sit down on the floor and pretend to play each instrument as it is included. They will suggest many more. On the last time it is sung they can each choose an instrument for themselves and make all the different noises at the same time.

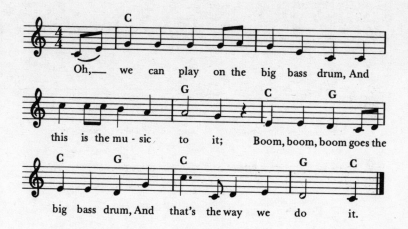

9 *Follow My Leader*

As I was walking down the street,
Heigh-ho, heigh-ho, heigh-ho,
A little friend I chanced to meet,
Heigh-ho, heigh-ho, heigh-ho!
Jiggety jig and away we go,
Away we go, away we go,
Jiggety jig and away we go,
Heigh-ho, heigh-ho, heigh-ho!

*Children skip round the room alone, then join hands
with a friend and skip holding hands.*

Variations:

A little dog I chanced to meet . . . scamper, scamper,
   scamper and away we go.
A very large horse . . . clippety clop and away we go.
A tiny little mouse . . . scurry, scurry, scurry and away
   we go.

                                                    EMM et al.

and anything else anyone likes to suggest.

The bear walked over the mountain,
The bear walked over the mountain,
The bear walked over the mountain,
   To see what he could see.

But all that he could see,
But all that he could see,
Was the other side of the mountain,
The other side of the mountain,
The other side of the mountain,
   Was all that he could see.

Children walk round room.

So he ran to another mountain,
He ran to another mountain,
He ran to another mountain,
   To see what he could see.

Turn round and run the other way.

But all that he could see, etc.

Followed by:
So he hopped to another mountain.
So he skipped to another mountain.
So he marched to another mountain.
So he tiptoed to another mountain.
So he climbed to another mountain.
So he jumped to another mountain.
So he clumped to another mountain.
So he stamped to another mountain.

or whatever the children like to suggest for themselves.

Sung to the tune of For he's a Jolly Good Fellow.

Did you ever see a lassie (laddie),
A lassie, a lassie;
Did you ever see a lassie
Go this way and that?

Go this way and that way,
And this way and that way.
Did you ever see a lassie
Go this way and that?

*During the first verse one child is in the ring and makes
some distinctive action while the others walk round.
The verse is sung again:*

Did you ever see a lassie, etc.
Who combed her hair like this?
Who washed her face like this?
Who put on her coat like this?

*while all the children copy the action. Another child
goes in the ring and the sequence starts again.*

Here we hop round the Mulberry Bush, etc.
    skip
    jump
    march
    crawl
    crab-walk
    bunny-hop

These are simple variations on Here we go round the Mulberry Bush (see page 62).

I went to school one morning and I walked like this,
Walked like this, walked like this.
I went to school one morning and I walked like this,
All on my way to school.

I saw a little robin and he hopped like this, etc.

I saw a shiny river and I splashed like this, etc.

I saw a little pony and he galloped like this, etc.

I saw a tall policeman and he stood like this, etc.

I heard the school bell ringing and I ran like this, etc.

Move around the room doing appropriate actions.

Capo 1st fret for chords in brackets

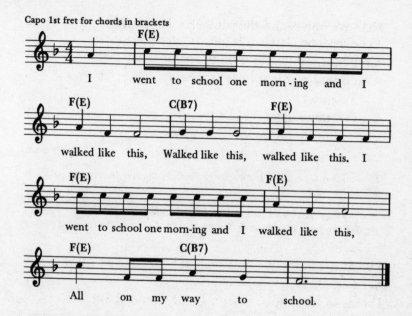

I went to school one morn-ing and I walked like this, Walked like this, walked like this. I went to school one morn-ing and I walked like this, All on my way to school.

Let everyone clap hands like me, (clap clap)
Let everyone clap hands like me, (clap clap)
Come on and join in with the game, (clap clap)
You'll find that it's always the same. (clap clap)

Let everyone stand up like me, etc.
                       sit down
                       turn round
                       jump up

*Plus anything else the children can do including pulling faces,
giggling, wiggling ears, (pretend) cleaning teeth, etc.*

Copy, copy,
Copy me do!
I do this,
Then you do it too!

Adult leader does all kinds of actions on 'I do this', e.g.

holds left ear with right hand
holds right ear with left hand
taps left foot
taps right foot
puts elbow on knee, etc.

*Coloured ribbon bands on hands and ankles can be helpful when children
progress to sorting out which hand/foot is which, but this needs some
care if the adult is facing the children.*

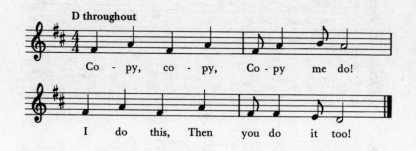

Words and music PATRICIA SEARS

If you're happy and you know it, clap your hands;
If you're happy and you know it, clap your hands;
If you're happy and you know it
And you want us all to know it,
If you're happy and you know it, clap your hands!

If you're happy and you know it, stamp your feet, etc.
       nod your head, etc.
       wave your hand, etc.
       shout 'We are!' etc.

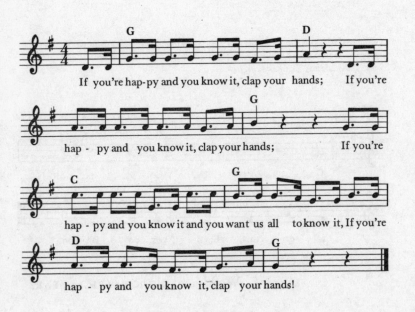

Other versions of this are:

If you're hungry and you know it, rub your tummy,
    etc.
If you're cross with everyone, pull a face, etc.
If you're cold and you know it, rub your arms, etc.

Or
If you want to do as I do, sit up straight, etc.

*Plus anything else the adult would like the children to do
such as clear up, sweep the floor, wipe the table, etc.*

We all clap hands together,
We all clap hands together,
We all clap hands together,
As children like to do.

Other verses:
We all stand up together, etc.

We all sit down together, etc.

We all stamp feet together, etc.

We all turn round together, etc.

Children like to make suggestions of their own, and the words may have to be fitted in quickly on one note.
Another common version finishes 'Because it's fun to do'.

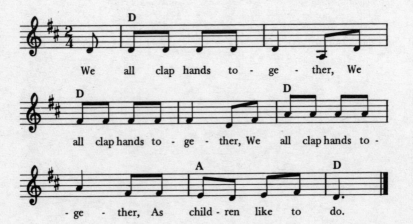

We all clap hands to - ge - ther, We all clap hands to - ge - ther, We all clap hands to - ge - ther, As child - ren like to do.

John Brown stamped his feet,
John Brown stamped his feet,
John Brown stamped his feet,
John Brown stamped both feet!

Followed by:
John Brown bent his ankles.
    slapped his knees.
    wiggled his bottom.
    puffed his chest out.
    shrugged his shoulders.
    nodded his head.
    raised his arms high.
    pointed with his elbows.
    clapped his hands.

EMM et al.

*For those who have enough puff, this can then be done in reverse
very quickly with one verse of the song for elbows, arms, head and
shoulders, another verse for chest, bottom, knees and ankles and
a last verse just for feet.*
*This is a variation of John Brown met a little Indian and the same
tune is used (see page 169).*

One finger, one thumb, keep moving,
One finger, one thumb, keep moving,
One finger, one thumb, keep moving,
We'll all be merry and bright!

One finger, one thumb, one arm, keep moving,
    etc.

One finger, one thumb, one arm, one leg, keep moving,
    etc.

One finger, one thumb, one arm, one leg, one nod of
    the head, keep moving,
etc.

Each part of the body is indicated by holding up as mentioned.
Some older children can then go on to:
Another finger, another thumb, keep moving, etc. but most adults
have had enough by the time they reach the end of the first round.

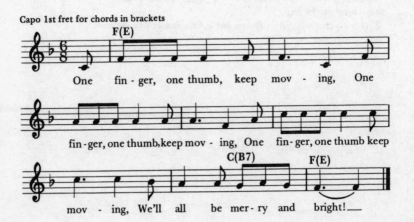

Heads and shoulders, knees and toes,
Knees and toes, knees and toes,
Heads and shoulders, knees and toes,
We all turn round together.

LINDA CHESTERMAN

Touch each part of the body as it is mentioned.

Teddy bear, Teddy bear, touch your nose,
Teddy bear, Teddy bear, touch your toes;
Teddy bear, Teddy bear, touch the ground,
Teddy bear, Teddy bear, turn around.

Teddy bear, Teddy bear, climb the stairs,
Teddy bear, Teddy bear, say your prayers;
Teddy bear, Teddy bear, turn off the light,
Teddy bear, Teddy bear, say Goodnight!

Follow the actions and then blow a big kiss on 'Goodnight!'

Roly poly, roly poly, up, up, up;
   Roll hands round each other moving upwards.
Roly poly, roly poly, down, down, down;
   Roll hands downwards.
Roly poly, roly poly, out, out, out;
   Roll hands away from you.
Roly poly, roly poly, in, in, in.
   Roll hands towards you.

Roly poly, ever so slowly . . . ever . . . so . . . slowly.
Roly poly, faster, faster, FASTER, FASTER!
Roly poly, ever so slowly, etc.

Roll fists round each other as the words suggest.

Big floppy scarecrows dangling along,
Dangling along, dangling along;
Big floppy scarecrows dangling along,
Dangling along just so!

Sly old foxes sidling along, etc.

Bobtailed rabbits hopping along, etc.

Heavy grey elephants lumbering along, etc.

EMM et al.

And anything else anyone likes to suggest.

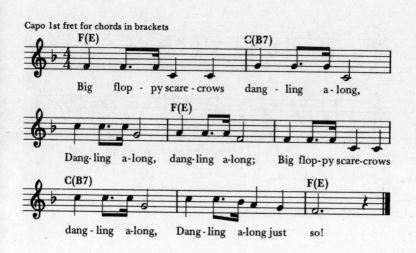

For echo songs the adult sings each phrase and children sing it back softly:

Echo,
> *Children sing it back.*

Mr Echo,
> *Children sing it back.*

Will you come and play?
> *Children sing it back.*

But not today.
> *Children sing it back.*

You're too far away!
> *Children sing it back.*

EMM et al.

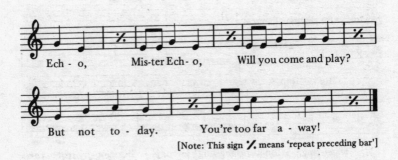

Ech-o,   Mis-ter Ech-o,   Will you come and play?

But not to-day.   You're too far a-way!

[Note: This sign ⁒ means 'repeat preceding bar']

Ally galoo, galoo,
Children sing it back.

Ally galoo, galay,
Children sing it back.

Ally galoo,
Children sing it back.

Ally galoo,
Children sing it back.

Ally galoo, galay–o!
Children sing it back.

EMM et al.

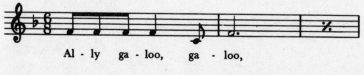

Al - ly ga - loo, ga - loo,

Al - ly ga - loo, ga - lay,   Al - ly ga - loo,

Al - ly ga - loo,   Al - ly ga - loo, ga - lay - o!

[Note: This sign ⁒ means 'repeat preceding bar or bars']

Other songs can be used in this way; see page 168, for example:

John Brown met a little Indian,
(echo) . . . He met a little Indian,
etc.
One little Indian boy.
(echo) . . . He met one little Indian boy.

EMM et al.

or Humpty Dumpty (see page 39).

10 In the Town

Safety Songs   211

The wheels on my bike go round like this,
Round like this, round like this;
The wheels on my bike go round like this,
All day long!

My feet on the pedals go round like this, etc.

The bell when it rings goes Ping! Ping! Ping! etc.

My breath when I ride goes Puff! Puff! Puff! etc.

*This is another version of The Wheels on the Bus
(see page 56).*

Here is the church,
   Interlace fingers with knuckles showing upwards.
Here is the steeple,
   Point index fingers up together to make a steeple.
Open the doors
   Turn hands over with fingers still interlaced.
And here are the people.
   Wriggle fingertips.
Here's the parson going upstairs,
   *Make a ladder with the left hand and walk right thumb and index finger
   up.*
And here he is a-saying his prayers.
   Put hands together as for prayer.

I'm driving in my car,
I'm driving in my car;
Peep-peep, toot-toot,
Peep-peep, toot-toot,
I'm driving in my car.

I'm driving very fast,
etc.

I'm driving very slow,
etc.

The lights have turned to red,
etc.
So I must stop the car.

The lights have turned to green,
    etc.
So I can go again.

This is sung to the tune of A Hunting We Will Go.

Here is a steamroller, rolling and rolling,
Ever so slowly, because of its load;
First it clanks up to the top of the hill,
Puffing and panting it has to stand still;
Then it rolls . . . all the way down!

Roll fists around each other slowly upwards, then down again
very fast on the last line.

Come to the station early in the morning,
See all the railway trains standing in a row;
Hear all the drivers starting up the engines,
Clickety-click, clickety-clack,

Say this slowly to begin with then repeat several times getting faster.

And away they go!

Come to the garage, etc.
See all the buses, etc.
Hear all the drivers, etc.
Rumble, rumble, rumble, etc.
And away they go!

Come to the seaside, etc.
See all the fishing boats, etc.
Hear all the captains, etc.
Splish, splash, splish, splash, etc.
And away they go!

Come to the airport, etc.
See all the aeroplanes, etc.
Hear all the pilots, etc.
Roar, roar, roar, etc.
And away they go!

This is another version of Down by the Station (see page 50) and is sung to the same tune.

Piggy on the railway
Picking up stones;
Along came an engine
And broke poor Piggy's bones.

'Oh!' said Piggy,
'That's not fair!'
'Oh!' said the engine driver,
'I don't care!'

*There are no specific actions to this rhyme . . . the children are too busy
waiting to say the 'I don't care!'*
*An older version of this rhyme starts 'Paddy on the railway' which makes
a good deal more sense historically speaking but children seem to enjoy
the slight dottiness of Piggy.*

There was a terrible collision on the railway line
When a poor cow didn't see the red light shine;
It happened quite a while ago . . .
They're still working on it now . . .
Sorting out the engine
From the poor old cow!

I had a little engine,
But it wouldn't go;
I had to push and push and push,
But still it wouldn't go.

I had a little motor-car,
But it wouldn't go;
I had to wind and wind and wind,
But still it wouldn't go.

I had a little aeroplane,
My aeroplane could fly;
I jumped right in, away I flew,
Right into the sky.

1st verse: Pretend to push hard.
2nd verse: Pretend to wind the handle.
3rd verse: Run round the room with arms outstretched.

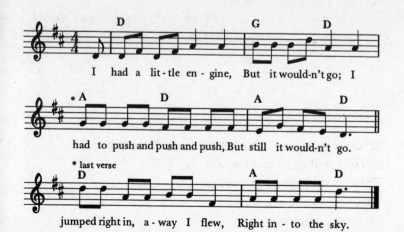

I had a lit-tle en-gine, But it would-n't go; I had to push and push and push, But still it would-n't go.

* last verse

jumped right in, a-way I flew, Right in-to the sky.

Aeroplanes, aeroplanes, all in a row;
Aeroplanes, aeroplanes, ready to go.
Hark! they're beginning to buzz and to hum,
Bzzzz;
Engines all working so come along, come.
Now we are flying up into the sky,
Faster and faster, oh, ever so high!

Gliders, gliders, away in the sky;
Gliders, gliders, they fly so high.
They don't have an engine so don't make a noise,
    Listen carefully and shake head.
They are quite silent –
Not like girls and boys.

Helicopters, helicopters, all in a row;
Helicopters, helicopters, ready to go.
They go whirling and twirling like large birds in flight,
And then the noise fades
As they twirl out of sight.

            LINDA CHESTERMAN (1st verse)
      KATIE ADAMSON (2nd and 3rd verses)

Ae - ro - planes, ae - ro - planes, all in a row;

Ae - ro - planes, ae - ro - planes, rea - dy to go.

Hark! they're be - gin - ning to buzz and to hum, Bzzzz;

En - gines all work - ing so come a - long, come.

Now we are fly - ing up in - to the sky,

Fast - er and fast - er, oh, ev - er so high!

Here comes a big red bus,
A big red bus, a big red bus;
Here comes a big red bus
To take us to the shops.

Here comes a minibus, etc. to take us all to school.

Here comes a motorcar, etc. to take us to the sea.

Here comes a taxi–cab, etc. to take us to the station.

Here comes a dustbin lorry, etc. to take away the
    rubbish.

Plus any other vehicles with which the children are familiar.
This is sung to the tune of Jack and Jill.

I went across the street one day,
And saw a car across the way,
        Or motor bike/bus/lorry/milk-float, etc.
And what do you think I heard it say?
Brrrm Brrrm Brrrm!
        The children will help out with the noises.

This is a variation of I went to Visit a Farm One Day (see page 70).

Ten little letters in a brown sack,
　　Hold up all fingers.
Along came the postman . . . Rat-a-tat tat;
　　Clap on Rat-a-tat tat.
He put two letters in (Anna)'s door,
　　Wriggle one finger on each hand.
Down they fell on to the floor.
　　Touch those two fingers on the floor.

Eight little letters, etc. and eventually . . .

No more letters in the brown sack,
No letters for you or for me;
So the postman puts his van away,
And goes home for his tea.

YVONNE BROADBENT and ELIZABETH MATTERSON

Clink, clink, clinketty clink,
The milkman's on his rounds I think;
Crunch, crunch come the milkman's feet,
Closer and closer along the street;
Then clink, clink, clinketty clink,
He's left our bottles of milk to drink.

CLIVE SANSOM

On the Bibblibonty Hill
Stands a Bibblibonty house;
In the Bibblibonty house
Are the Bibblibonty people;
The Bibblibonty people
Have Bibblibonty children;
The Bibblibonty children
Take a Bibblibonty sup
With a Bibblibonty spoon
From a Bibblibonty cup.

ROSE FYLEMAN

Two fat gentlemen met in a lane,
Bowed most politely, bowed once again.
How do you do,
How do you do,
And how do you do again?

Two thin ladies met in a lane, etc.

Two tall policemen met in a lane, etc.

Two little schoolboys met in a lane, etc.

Two little babies met in a lane, etc.

1st verse: Bend thumbs. 2nd verse: Bend forefingers.
3rd verse: Bend middle fingers. 4th verse: Bend ring fingers.
5th verse: Bend little fingers.

BOYCE and BARTLETT

Round and round the village,
Round and round the village,
Round and round the village,
As we have done before.

In and out the windows, etc.

Take yourself a partner, etc.

Bow (curtsy) before you leave her (him), etc.

1st verse: One child skips round outside the ring of children.
2nd verse: He then skips in and out under their raised arms.
3rd verse: He takes a partner and dances with her in the ring.
4th verse: He bows to her then rejoins the ring. She then repeats the game.
Use the traditional tune below.

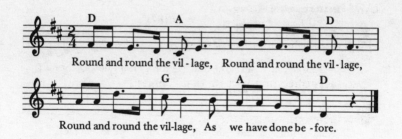

Run, run up the hill,
Run, run down the hill;
Run, run round the hill,
Till we're home!

Then:
Skip/hop/crawl/slither/jump/whistle/sing, etc.
and when everyone has had enough . . .

Puff, puff, up the hill,
etc. (*very slowly*)
Till we're home!

EMM et al.

Another variation of this is to 'run to' different places, e.g.
Run, run up the street/up the lane/up to town/off to (and back from)
school.

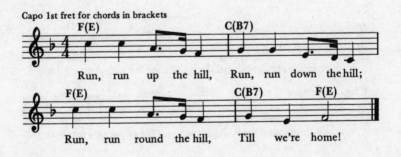

Capo 1st fret for chords in brackets

Safety Songs

Watch that truck, watch that truck
Rolling down the road;
It can't stop as fast as us
With its heavy load!

Chorus:
Crossing roads, crossing roads
On our way to school;
We must learn the Green Cross Code
It is our golden rule!

Watch that bus, watch that bus
Rushing down the road;
It can't stop as fast as us
With its heavy load!

Repeat chorus

Plus any other verses the children suggest.

from ROSPA'S TUFTY ROAD SAFETY SCHEME

Sung to the tune of Jingle Bells.

Stop! Look! and Think!
Stop! Look! and Think!
Before you cross the road,
Before you cross the road;
You must use your eyes and use your ears,
You must use your eyes and use your ears,
And if no bus or car appears . . .
THEN you can cross the road!

from ROSPA'S TUFTY ROAD SAFETY SCHEME

Sung to the tune of Three Blind Mice.

Stop says the red light,
Go says the green,
Change says the amber one
Winking in between;
That's what they say
And that's what they mean;
If we all obey them
We are sure to be seen.

from ROSPA'S TUFTY ROAD SAFETY SCHEME

In a farmyard near a roadway,
Lived some ducklings one to nine;
They also had a little sister,
And her name was Clementine.

Through the gateway went these ducklings,
On a day so very fine;
They were followed by their sister,
Little sister Clementine.

They all shouted to their sister,
To their sister Clementine;
Say your Green Cross Code little sister,
Do be careful, Clementine.

But she dashed into the roadway,
Never heeding brothers nine;
And a lorry drove right over her,
Foolish foolish Clementine!

Do remember, little children,
Whether it be wet or fine;
You must always use the Green Cross Code,
Don't get squashed like Clementine.

from ROSPA'S TUFTY ROAD SAFETY SCHEME

This is sung to the tune of O my Darling Clementine.

Two little eyes to look all around,
Two little ears to hear any sound;
Two little hands to hold hands tight,
Two little feet to walk left or right;
Two little lips to say BEWARE!
One little child to cross the road with care!

SHEILA GROVE

This can be sung to the tune of Twinkle, Twinkle Little Star.

One man went to mow,
Went to mow a meadow;
One man and his dog, Woof! Woof!
Went to mow a meadow.

Two men went to mow, etc.

Three men, etc.

Four men, etc.

This may be played as a finger counting game, or with children acting as the men.

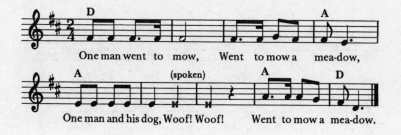

Oats and beans and barley grow,
Oats and beans and barley grow,
But not you nor I nor anyone know
How oats and beans and barley grow.

First the farmer sows his seed,
Then he stands and takes his ease,
Stamps his feet and claps his hands
And turns him round to view the land.

*During the first verse the children skip round in a ring. During the second verse
they do the appropriate actions. (There are more verses to this but they are not so
attractive to small children as the first two.)*

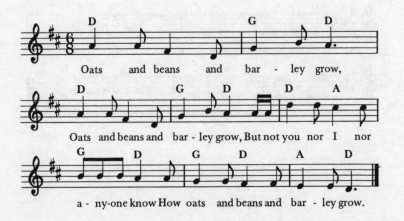

Oats and beans and bar - ley grow,
Oats and beans and bar - ley grow, But not you nor I nor
a - ny-one know How oats and beans and bar - ley grow.

Little piggy-wig on the farm close by,
All by himself ran away from the sty.
The dog said 'Woof',
The cow said 'Moo',
The sheep said 'Baa',
The dove said 'Coo';
Little piggy-wig began to cry,
And as fast as he could he ran back to the sty!

The turkey is a funny bird,
Its head goes bobble-bobble;
And all he knows is just one word . . .
And that is
GOBBLE-GOBBLE!

John Brown's tractor had a puncture in its tyre, Ssss
John Brown's tractor had a puncture in its tyre, Ssss
John Brown's tractor had a puncture in its tyre, Ssss
So he mended it with chewing-gum!

Chewy, chewy, chewy, chewing-gum,
Chewy, chewy, chewy, chewing-gum,
Chewy, chewy, chewy, chewing-gum,
So he mended it with chewing-gum!

MARGARET GRAY and the
BELFAST NURSERY SCHOOL TEACHERS

Small children enjoy this song as it is — but older children can manage to miss off a word each time they repeat the verse again, clapping hands to fill in the rhythm of the missing word.

John Brown's trac - tor had a punc-ture in its tyre, Ssss

John Brown's trac - tor had a punc-ture in its tyre, Ssss

John Brown's trac - tor had a punc-ture in its tyre, Ssss So he

mend-ed it with chew-ing - gum! Chew - y, chew-y, chew-y,

chew - ing - gum, Chew - y, chew - y, chew - y,

chew - ing gum, Chew - y, chew - y, chew - y,

chew - ing-gum, So he mend- ed it with chew-ing - gum!

Cows in the kitchen, Moo Moo Moo,
Cows in the kitchen, Moo Moo Moo,
Cows in the kitchen, Moo Moo Moo,
What shall we do, Tom Farmer?

Ducks in the dustbin, Quacker-de-doo, etc.

Cat's in the cupboard, Dog is too, etc.

Pig's in the garden, eating the roots, etc.

'Chase them away then, Shoo Shoo Shoo, etc.
That's what we'll do,' said Tom Farmer!

*For cows hold up hands to top of the head like horns, for ducks use one hand
like a beak quacking, for cat indicate whiskers, for dog use hand and arm like
a wagging tail, for pig indicate a curly tail and do the Shoo-ing with both
hands.*
This is sung to the tune for Skip to my Lou (see page 305).

Five brown eggs in a nest of hay . . .
One yellow chick popped out to play.

Four brown eggs in a nest of hay . . .
Another yellow chick cheep–cheeped Good day.

Three brown eggs in a nest of hay . . .
Crack went another one, Hip hooray.

Two brown eggs in a nest of hay . . .
One more chick pecked his shell away.

One brown egg in a nest of hay . . .
The last yellow chick popped out to say
Happy Easter

This can be sung to the tune of Five Currant Buns if the rhythm is slightly adapted (see page 51).

Five fluffy chicks
Were pecking in the sun,
The old fox came
And he caught one!

*Fingers of one hand for chicks, use the other for the fox
and grab the chicks.*

Four fluffy chicks
Were pecking in the sun,
The fox came again
And caught another one!

Three fluffy chicks, etc.

No fluffy chicks left
To peck in the sun,
The farmer came out with his gun,
The old fox went off
Run Run Run!

EMM et al.

Higgledy Piggledy, my black hen,
She lays eggs for gentlemen;
Sometimes nine and sometimes ten.
Higgledy Piggledy, my black hen.

Chick, chick, chick, chick, chicken,
Lay a little egg for me!
Chick, chick, chick, chick, chicken,
I want one for my tea!
I haven't had one since breakfast
And now it's half past three
So . . . Chick, chick, chick, chick, chicken,
Lay a little egg for me!

FRANCIS, DAY, HUNTER

The farmer's dog's at my back door,
His name is Bobby Bingo;
B–I–N–G–O, B–I–N–G–O, B–I–N–G–O,
His name is Bobby Bingo!

The farmer's dog lies on the mat, etc.

The farmer's dog's sitting on my chair, etc.

The farmer's dog has eaten my cheese, etc.

*This is a ring game . . . the chosen Bingo goes into the middle and the other
children walk round singing. At the end of the verse 'Bingo' points to one
child for B, the next for I, etc. and the child who is O becomes the next Bingo.
For very young children who cannot manage walking round in a ring reverse the
movement . . . the children sit in a ring and 'Bingo' does the moving round.*

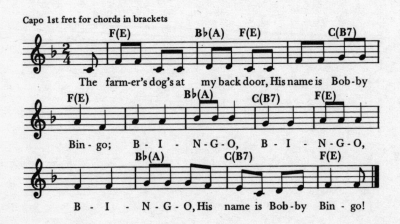

Foxy's creeping round the farm,
> *'Creep' the right hand on the floor.*

Trying to catch the chickens.
Up jumps the farmer with his gun, Bang! Bang!
> *Raise left hand for farmer.*

Look at poor old Foxy run!
> *Right hand runs behind back.*

He runs away and hides
And home goes Farmer Jones;
> *Hide other hand.*

Then old Foxy, he creeps back
To get those chicken bones!

12 In the Garden and in the Country

A tiny, tiny worm
Wriggled along the ground;
It wriggled along like this
Without a sound.

It came to a tiny hole,
A tiny hole in the ground;
It wriggled right inside
Without a sound.

WYN DANIEL EVANS

Wriggle right index finger along the floor.
Make the hole with left thumb and index finger.

Under a stone where the earth was firm,
I found a wiggly, wriggly worm;
  Use forefinger for worm and cover with other hand.
'Good morning,' I said.
'How are you today?'
  Uncover the forefinger.
But the wiggly worm just wriggled away!
  Wriggle the forefinger up the other arm.

I saw a slippery, slithery snake
Slide through the grasses, making them shake.
Right index finger weaves through fingers of left hand.

He looked at me with his beady eye.
Right index finger and thumb make ring round eye.

'Go away from my pretty green garden,' said I.
Make shooing movements with left hand

'Sssssss,' said the slippery, slithery snake,
As he slid through the grasses making them shake.
Repeat first movement.

There's a worm at the bottom of my garden
And his name is Wiggly Woo.
There's a worm at the bottom of my garden
And all that he can do –
Is wiggle all night
And wiggle all day,
Whatever else the people do say;
There's a worm at the bottom of my garden
And his name is Wiggly, Wig-Wig-Wiggly,
Wig-Wig-Wiggly Woo-oo!

DAVID EVANS

Capo 1st fret for chords in brackets

There's a worm at the bot - tom of my gar - den And his name is Wig - gl - y Woo. There's a worm at the bot-tom of my gar- den And all that he can do — Is wig-gle all night And wig-gle all day, What-ev-er else the peo-ple do say; There's a worm at the bot - tom of my gar - den And his name is Wig - gl - y, Wig — Wig — Wig - gl - y, Wig — Wig — Wig - gl - y Woo - oo!

'Who's that tickling my back?'
Said the wall;
'Me,' said a small caterpillar.
'I'm learning to crawl!'

IAN SERRAILLIER

What do you suppose?
A bee sat on my nose!
> *Land the tips of forefinger and thumb on the bridge of the nose.*

Then what do you think?
He gave me a wink.
> *Wink one eye.*

And said, 'I beg your pardon,
I thought you were the garden!'

A hive for a honey-bee,
A kennel for a dog;
A hutch for a rabbit
And a pond for a frog;
A stable for a donkey,
A hole for a mouse . . .
But I would like a caravan
For my special house!

Ladybird, Ladybird, fly away home;
Your house is on fire, and your children all gone;
All but the youngest, whose name is Anne,
And she hid under the frying pan.

This can be sung to the tune of Pussycat, Pussycat, Where Have you Been?

Five little leaves so bright and gay
Were dancing about on a tree one day.
The wind came blowing through the town
Whooooooooo . . . Whooooooooo
And one little leaf came tumbling down.

Four little leaves, etc.

Use fingers to represent leaves, and blow hard through cupped hands to make the noise of the wind.
This can be sung to the tune of Five Little Ducks (see page 46).

I went to the garden and dug up the ground,
Dug up the ground, dug up the ground;
I went to the garden and dug up the ground,
On Sunday in the morning.

I went to the garden and raked the soil fine, etc.
On Monday in the morning.

. . . sowed all my seeds, On Tuesday etc.
. . . watered the ground, On Wednesday, etc.
. . . scared off the birds, On Thursday, etc.
. . . chased off the cats, On Friday, etc.
. . . picked up the slugs, On Saturday, etc.
. . . saw some green shoots, On Sunday, etc.

I went to the garden and picked all my flowers, etc.
After (????) Sundays in the morning.
Ask the children about how many Sundays they think it will take.

EMM et al

I went to the gar-den and dug up the ground, Dug up the

ground, dug up the ground; I went to the gar-den and

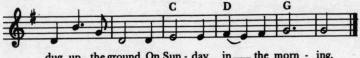

dug up the ground, On Sun-day in — the morn-ing.

Four scarlet berries
Left upon the tree.
'Thanks,' said the blackbird,
'These will do for me!'
He ate numbers one and two,
Then ate number three;
When he'd eaten number four,
There was none to see!

MARY VIVIAN

Five little sparrows I can see,
Five little sparrows, sitting on a tree,
One of them flew home for his tea;
How many sparrows left for me to see?

Four little sparrows, etc.

One little sparrow I can see,
One little sparrow left on the tree;
Said he, 'I think I'll just stay here,
They won't have left any tea for me!'

EMM et al.

Little Robin Redbreast
Perched up in a tree;
Up went Pussycat
Down came he!
Down followed Pussycat,
Away the robin ran,
Said little Robin Redbreast,
'Catch me if you can!'

This can be sung to the tune of Goosey Goosey Gander
if the rhythm is adapted slightly to fit these words.

Five wood-pigeons sitting on a wall,
Two were very big, three were very small;
Along came the wind and caused one to fall,
That left four wood-pigeons sitting on a wall.

Four wood-pigeons etc.
  Decide on whether they are large or small.

One wood-pigeon sitting on the wall,
Left on his own, with no other bird at all;
So he flew off, before HE should fall
And that left no wood-pigeons sitting on the wall.

This is sung to the tune for Ten Green Bottles.

Two little blackbirds sitting in the sun,
Wriggle two forefingers.
One flew away and then there was one.
Hide one finger.
One little blackbird, very black and small,
Wriggle other finger.
He flew away and then there was the wall.
Hide other finger.
One little brick wall, lonely in the lane,
Hands to eyes, peeping through fingers.
Waiting for the blackbirds to come and sing again.

In a dark, dark wood there's a dark, dark house
In a dark, dark house there's a dark, dark room,
In a dark, dark room there's a dark, dark cupboard
In a dark, dark cupboard there's a dark, dark box,
In the dark, dark box there's a (????)

*There are many variations of what is in the box from ghosts who go Whoo-oo
to mice who go Squea–k. If the children are allowed to say what is in the box
no one is going to have nightmares about their own choice at least.*

There's a wide-eyed owl
  Forefingers and thumbs round eyes.
With a pointed nose,
  Forefinger and thumb make a point.
He has pointed ears
  Clenched hands, forefingers up for ears.
And claws for toes:
  Make hands into claws.
He sits in a tree
And looks at you;
  Circles round eyes again.
Then flaps his wings and says,
  Hands to chest and 'flap' elbows.
'Tu-whit, tu-whoo!'
  Hands cup mouth to hoot.

This little rabbit said, 'Let's play.'
This little rabbit said, 'In the hay.'
This little rabbit said, 'I see a man with a gun.'
This little rabbit said, 'That isn't fun.'
This little rabbit said, 'I'm off for a run.'
BANG went the gun
And they all ran away,
And they never came back for a year and a day!

Point to all fingers and thumb in turn, clap hands on BANG and hide fingers behind back.

If you go down to the woods today,
You're sure of a big surprise.
If you go down to the woods today
You'd better go in disguise!
For every bear that ever there was
Will gather there for certain because
Today's the day the Teddy Bears have their picnic.

Every Teddy Bear who's been good
Is sure of a treat today.
There'll be lots of marvellous things to eat
And wonderful games to play!
Beneath the trees where nobody sees
They'll play hide-and-seek as long as they please
Because that's the way the Teddy Bears have their
    picnic.

Picnic time for Teddy Bears,
Those little Teddy Bears are having a lovely time today;
Watch them, catch them unawares.
And see them picnic on their holiday.
You'll see them gaily gad about,
They love to play and shout, they never have any cares;
At six o'clock their mummies and daddies will take
    them home to bed
Because they're tired little Teddy Bears.

           JOHN BRATTON and **JIMMY KENNEDY**

Between the valley and the hill
> *Interlock fingers, palms up for valley, knuckles up for hill.*

There sat a little hare;
> *Clench hands forefingers up for ears.*

He nibbled at the grass until
The ground was nearly bare:
> *Right hand 'nibbles' over clenched left hand.*

And when the ground was nearly bare,
He rested in the sun;
> *Flat right hand rests on flat left hand.*

A hunter came and saw him there
And shot him with his gun!
> *Left hand, two fingers extended 'shoots' right hand, two loud claps.*

The poor hare thought he must be dead,
> *Head down, hands over eyes*

But wonderful to say,
He found he was ALIVE instead!
> *Sit up, look round, twitch nose.*

And quickly ran away.
> *Right hand runs up left hand and arm to shoulder and behind neck.*

Words ROSE FYLEMAN
Music EMM et al.

Capo 1st fret for chords in brackets

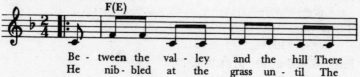

Be - tween the val - ley and the hill There
He nib - bled at the grass un - til The

sat a lit - tle hare;
ground was near - ly bare: And when the ground was near-ly bare, He

rest - ed in the sun; A hun - ter came and

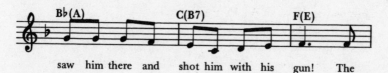

saw him there and shot him with his gun! The

poor hare thought he must be dead, But won-der-ful to say, He

found he was A- LIVE in- stead! And quick-ly ran a - way.

Ten little squirrels sat on a tree.
  Show ten fingers.
The first two said, 'Why, what do we see?'
  Hold up thumbs.
The next two said, 'A man with a gun.'
  Hold up forefingers.
The next two said, 'Let's run, let's run.'
  Hold up middle fingers.
The next two said, 'Let's hide in the shade.'
  Hold up ring fingers.
The next two said, 'Why, we're not afraid.'
  Hold up the little fingers.
But BANG went the gun, and away they all ran.
  Clap loudly and hide all fingers.

13 Things We See Near Water

Row, boys, row,
As up the stream we go;
With a long pull,
And a strong pull!
Row, boys, row.

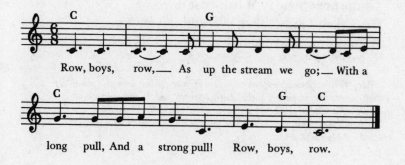

Down by the river where the green grass grows
Kneels (Mary Wilson) washing her clothes.
She sings, she sings, she sings so sweet;
She calls to her playmates across the street.

'Playmates, playmates, won't you come to tea?
Come next Sunday at half-past three.
Tea cakes, Lardy cakes, everything you'll see,
If you come next Sunday at half-past three.'

*'Mary Wilson' kneels in the middle of the ring of children who skip round her.
She chooses two playmates at the 'half-past three' and the three of them
decide what kind of cakes they are going to have, tell this to the other
children and they all sing the last two lines. An adult then chooses the next
child to be in the middle.*

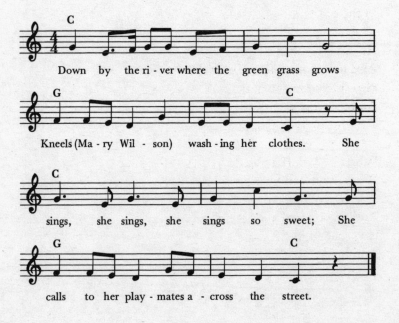

*The first verse is the chorus and this part is sung at the end of each
succeeding verse with words slightly changed. The new lines to each verse
are sung to the first two bars of the tune, repeated as many times as necessary.*

A little green frog
Lived under a log
Near a pond,
By the fence,
In the garden.

He croaked in the dark
And he croaked in the light;
That little green frog
Who lived under a log
Near a pond,
By the fence,
In the garden.

He croaked all the day
And he croaked all the night;
He croaked in the dark
And he croaked in the light;
That little green frog, etc.

When he swam he went SPLASH!
When he dived he went SPLOSH!
And he croaked all the day
And he croaked all the night;
He croaked in the dark
And he croaked in the light;
That little green frog, etc.

The people who lived there
Were driven quite mad
By the noise of the frog
Who lived under the log;
Who swam and went SPLASH!
And dived and went SPLOSH!
Who croaked all the day
And croaked all the night;
Who croaked in the dark
And croaked in the light;
That little green frog, etc.

In the Autumn he went . . .
They never knew where;
And they missed all the noise
Of their old friend the frog,
Who swam and went SPLASH!
And dived and went SPLOSH!
Who croaked all the day
And croaked all the night;
Who croaked in the dark
And croaked in the light;
That little green frog
Who left his big log
Near the pond,
By the fence,
In the garden!

ELIZABETH MATTERSON

Capo 1st fret for chords in brackets

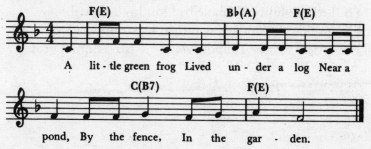

Five little froggies sitting on a well
One looked up and down he fell!
Froggies jumped high,
Froggies jumped low;
And four little froggies searched high and low . . .
. . . But they couldn't find him!
Say the last line.

Four little froggies, etc.

No little froggies sitting on the well,
Because they all looked up and down they fell!
Their mother jumped high,
Their mother jumped low;
The mother frog searched high and low . . .
. . . And she found all of them!

Sing to the tune of Ten Green Bottles, adapting the rhythm to fit these words.

Little Tommy Tadpole began to weep and wail,
For little Tommy Tadpole had lost his little tail!
His mother did not know him as he sat upon a log,
For little Tommy Tadpole was now Mr Thomas Frog!

Sing to the tune of I had a Little Nut Tree.

She sailed away on a lovely summer's day
On the back of a crocodile;
'You see,' said she, 'he's as tame as tame can be,
A-floating down the Nile!'
The croc winked his eye as she waved her friends
    goodbye
Wearing a happy smile;
By the end of the ride the lady was inside,
And the smile was on the crocodile!

She sailed a - way on a love- ly sum-mer's day On the

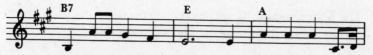

back of a croc - o - dile;   'You   see,' said she, 'he's as

tame as tame can be,   A   float - ing down the Nile!'   The

croc winked his   eye   as she waved her friends good-bye ——

Wear- ing a hap - py smile;   By the end of the ride the

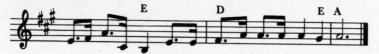

la - dy was in - side, and the smile was on the croc-o - dile!

The big ship sails through the Alley, Alley O;
Alley, Alley O; Alley, Alley O,
The big ship sails through the Alley, Alley O
On the last day of September.

The Captain said, 'It will never, never do;
Never, never do; never, never do,' etc.

The big ship sank to the bottom of the sea;
The bottom of the sea; the bottom of the sea, etc.

We all dip our heads in the deep blue sea;
The deep blue sea; the deep blue sea, etc.

All the children hold hands in a long line. One of the end children puts his arm up against a wall to make an arch. The child at the other end of the line goes under the arch followed by the others. As the last one goes through the child touching the wall is twisted round so that his arms are crossed. The 'leader' of the line then goes through the arch made by the child touching the wall and his neighbour so that the neighbour twists round as the last child goes through. This is repeated using the first verse only until all the children have crossed arms. The ring then joins up by the first and last child joining crossed hands. During the second verse all shake their heads gravely. For the third verse they slowly squat down and rise again, still holding crossed hands. For the fourth verse they all bend their heads down as low as possible, repeating until the end of the verse.

Capo 1st fret for chords in brackets

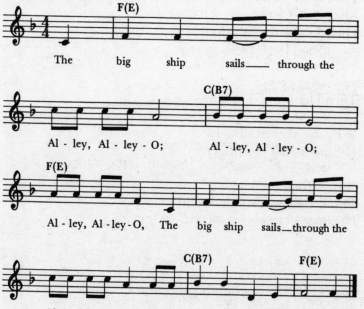

The big ship sails⸺ through the

Al - ley, Al - ley - O; Al - ley, Al - ley - O;

Al - ley, Al - ley - O, The big ship sails⸺through the

Al - ley, Al - ley O On the last day of Sep - tem - ber.

One, two, three, four, five,
Count on fingers.
Once I caught a fish alive;
Wriggle hand like a fish.
Six, seven, eight, nine, ten,
Count fingers.
Then I let him go again.
Pretend to throw fish back.
Why did you let him go?
Because he bit my finger so!
Shake hand violently.
Which finger did he bite?
This little finger on the right!
Hold up little finger of right hand.

Four little fishes swimming out to sea,
One met a shark! . . .
And then there were three.

Three little fishes wondering what to do,
One hid in a great big shell . . .
And then there were two.

Two little fishes looking for some fun,
One chased after a wave . . .
And that left only one.

One little fish with all his friends gone,
Went back home to find his mum . . .
And that left none!

GLENDA BANKS

Going fishing in the deep blue sea,
Catching fishes for my tea;
Catch another for my brother,
One! Two! Three!

Repeat with different second lines:

Crabs from the rock-pool for my tea, etc.

Lobsters in the lobster-pot for my tea, etc.

Shrimps in the shrimping net for my tea, etc.

ALISON WELLS and ELIZABETH MATTERSON
See page 24 for music.

The fisherman rows his boat along,
His arms are beautifully brown and strong.
He throws his net into the sea
And catches a big fish as long as me!

*Children sit in a circle to 'row' and throw the net then stretch out
as long as possible on the floor. The adult chooses the most stretched-
out child (not necessarily the biggest one).*

Capo 1st fret for chords in brackets

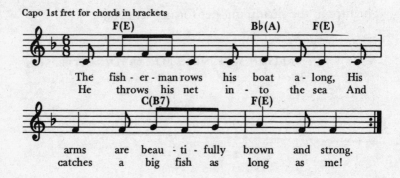

The fish - er - man rows his boat a - long, His
He throws his net in - to the sea And

arms are beau - ti - fully brown and strong.
catches a big fish as long as me!

Three jellyfish, three jellyfish,
Three jellyfish sitting on a rock.
One fell off! ... Oooooo, oooooo.

Two jellyfish, etc.

One jellyfish, etc.

No jellyfish, etc.

Then:
Three jellyfish, three jellyfish,
Three jellyfish swimming in the sea.
They all jumped on ... HOORAY!

JEAN CHADWICK

Use fingers to show how many jellyfish.

Additional variation: older children can add to this the second time around by singing:

Three wobbly jellyfish, three wobbly jellyfish, etc.
And the next time:
Three wibbly-wobbly jellyfish, three wibbly-wobbly jellyfish, etc.

Seagull, seagull, sit on the shore,
Sit on the shore, sit on the shore;
Seagull, seagull, sit on the shore,
Sail away my *Santi-Anna*.

Puffin, puffin, follow the ship, etc.
Sail away my *Santi-Anna*.

Penguin, penguin, swim in the sea, etc.
Sail away my *Santi-Anna*.

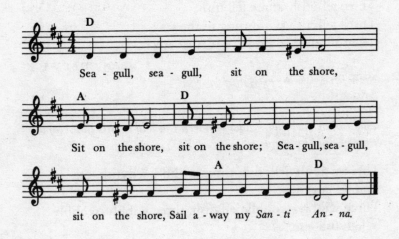

There was a little turtle and he lived in a box,
He swam in a puddle
And he climbed on the rocks;
He snapped at a mosquito –
He snapped at a flea –
He snapped at a minnow –
And he snapped at ME!
He caught the mosquito –
He caught the flea –
He caught the minnow –
But he didn't catch ME!

VACHEL LINDSAY

Slippery Sam was a slippery seal
And a slippery seal was he;
He slithered and slid to the sandy shore
Then he slipped back into the sea.

Water in bottles, water in pans,
Water in kettles, water in cans;
It's always the shape of whatever it's in,
Bucket or kettle, or bottle or tin.

RODNEY BENNETT

Sing to the tune of On Top of Old Smokey.

Gentle Animals

Five little mice came out to play
Gathering crumbs up on their way;
Out came pussy-cat
Sleek and black,
Four little mice went scampering back!

Four little mice, etc.

Use the fingers on one hand for mice and the other for the cat.

Hippety-hop, hippety-hay,
Five little bunnies went out to play;
Hippety-hippety-hop, hay-hay,
One little bunny ran away!

Four little bunnies, etc.

Hippety-hop, hippety-hay,
No little bunnies to go out to play;
Because they've all run away, hay-hay,
Because they've all run away!

John Brown had a little puppy dog,
John Brown had a little puppy dog,
John Brown had a little puppy dog
And he took him for a walk each day!

This can go on as long as anyone can find more suggestions, e.g.

. . . had a little kitten . . . she chased her tail all day.
. . . had a little hamster . . . he hid in his nest all day.
. . . had a little rabbit . . . she twitched her whiskers all
   day.
. . . had a little tortoise . . . he ambled round all day.

This is sung to the tune of John Brown met a little Indian (see page 168).

How much is that doggie in the window?
The one with the waggly tail;
How much is that doggie in the window?
I do hope that he is for sale!

BOB MERRILL

Oh where, oh where has my little dog gone?
Oh where, oh where can he be? With his ears so short
   and his tail so long,
Oh where, oh where is he?

I saw a little blue-bird and he hopped like this,
  'Hop' two forefingers on knee.
Hopped like this,
Hopped like this;
I saw a little blue-bird and he hopped like this,
When I was going to school!

I saw a cheeky sparrow and he cheeped like this, etc.
  (*cheep-cheep*)
 I saw a white dove and he cooed like this, etc. (*coo-coo*)
I saw a little wagtail and he wiggled like this, etc. (*wiggle
   bottom*)

*This is a very useful and flexible variation of I Went to School One Morning (see
page 182) and is sung to the same tune. It can also be used for farm babies or zoo
animals, e.g.*
I saw a little calf and he mooed like this, etc.
When I went to the farmyard.

Poor little bird in a bamboo cage,
Will you sing a song for me
If I come and set you free?
Who's behind you, can you tell,
Who's behind you?
     Other child says:
Tell me now!

*Children sit in a ring, one sits on adult's lap with the adult's hand
covering her eyes. They sing the song and at the appropriate point another
child comes up behind the 'bird' and says, 'Tell me now!' If the 'bird'
guesses correctly he changes places and the other child becomes the bird.*

I have a little spider,
And I'm very fond of him;
He climbs on to my shoulder,
And then up to my chin;
He crawls down my arm,
And then down my leg;
Now he's a tired little spider
So I put him into bed.

One hand does a 'spider crawl' up to shoulder, chin etc.
and then he is put to bed in a cupped other hand.

Little Arabella Miller
Found a woolly caterpillar.
First it crawled upon her mother,
Then upon her baby brother;
All said, 'Arabella Miller,
Take away that caterpillar.'

ANN ELLIOTT

Pretend to pick up the caterpillar; walk fingers of right hand up the left arm then vice versa; pretend to put the caterpillar down.

Lit - tle Ar - a - bel - la Mil - ler Found a wool - ly cat - er - pil - lar. First it crawled up - on her mo - ther, Then up - on her ba - by bro - ther; All said, 'Ar - a - bel - la Mil - ler, Take a - way that cat - er - pil - lar.'

There's a very furry caterpillar
Crawling up that tree;
I hope that furry caterpillar
Doesn't crawl on me!

There's a hedgehog on the grass,
Do you think he'll let me pass?
Or will he curl up in a ball,
     Curl up tightly with arms over heads.
Pretending I'm not here at all!

Frogs jump, caterpillars hump;
Worms wriggle, insects tiggle;
Rabbits hop, horses clop;
Snakes slide, seagulls glide;
Mice creep, deer leap;
Puppies bounce, kittens pounce;
Lions stalk . . . but I WALK!

EVELYN BAYER

Fierce Animals

Walking through the jungle,
What do you think we'll see
If we hear a noise like this:
Roar! Roar!
What do you think it will be?

EMM et al.

*Ask children to whisper suggestions to adult and see if
the others can guess what it is that is making that noise.*

There's a great big bear,
Sleeping over there;
Who's going to hide his/her honey?
            Children take turns to hide the honey-pot.
Wake up Mr/Mrs Bear,
Go and find your honey!

*The child who is the sleeping 'bear' wakes up and has to search for the honey-pot.
Older children can play the old game of Warm, warmer or Cold, colder but very
young children will help by making comments on the bear's progress.*

Look at the terrible crocodile,
I-oh, I-oh, I-oh.
He's swimming down the River Nile,
I-oh, I-oh, I-oh.

See his jaws are open wide,
I-oh, I-oh, I-oh.
A dear little fish is swimming inside . . .
Oh, no he isn't – (*This line is said softly*)
He's going the other way!

Put palms flat together and weave them about for the crocodile. Keep the hands touching at the wrist while finger tips flap apart in time to the refrain of 'I-oh'. Use a wriggling finger for the little fish.

Please Mr Crocodile,
May we cross the water,
To see your ugly daughter
Floating on the water
Like a cup and saucer?

The crocodile answers:
Yes, if you're dressed in (blue).

All the children line up on one side of the space and chant to the
'crocodile' who can choose what he will allow in the way of clothes.
Anyone who does not have this colour or garment has to try to rush or sneak
by him to the other side. The first person he catches is the next
'crocodile'.
Some discretion is needed as to whether a group is old enough to play this game.

If you should meet a crocodile,
Don't take a stick and poke him;
Ignore the welcome in his smile,
Be careful not to stroke him!
For as he sleeps upon the Nile
He thinner gets and thinner;
So whenever you meet a crocodile
He's ready for his dinner!

I'm a lion in the forest and I'm looking for my tea.
Oh, please, Mr Lion . . . don't eat me!

I'm a lion in the forest, and I must have some meat.
Oh, please, Mr Lion . . . I'm not the one to eat!

I'm a lion in the forest, and I've waited LONG
   ENOUGH!
Oh, please, Mr Lion . . . you'll find I'm very tough!

BARBARA IRESON

Mr Smith the Keeper has ten lions in his Zoo,
Mr Smith the Keeper has ten lions in his Zoo,
Mr Smith the Keeper has ten lions in his Zoo,
And he has to feed them every day!

Then:
Nine tigers, eight zebras, seven giraffes, six leopards, five
monkeys, four camels, three hippos, two parrots . . .
and an ostrich.

Sung to the tune of John Brown's Tractor (see page 221).

Lord Longleat had a game reserve,
E–I–E–I–O;
And on this reserve he had some lions,
E–I–E–I–O:
There were –
Big lions, little lions, little lions, big lions,
Fat lions, thin lions, thin lions, fat lions;
Lord Longleat had a game reserve,
E–I–E–I–O

Followed by:
Tigers, jaguars, monkeys, three–toed sloths, etc.

During the big, little, fat, thin indicate these with hands.
For children with enough puff there could also be tall lions, short lions,
happy lions, grumpy lions, etc.
Sung to the tune of Old MacDonald had a Farm (see page 65).

There are monkeys and bears and a big kangaroo,
Lions and tigers and elephants too;
Pandas and camels and a talking cockatoo . . .
And lots more animals live in the zoo.

There are bisons, okapi and even a gnu,
An elk and an eland and a rhino or two;
There are birds, there are fish, there are insects too . . .
I visit them all and say 'How do you do?'

ELIZABETH MATTERSON

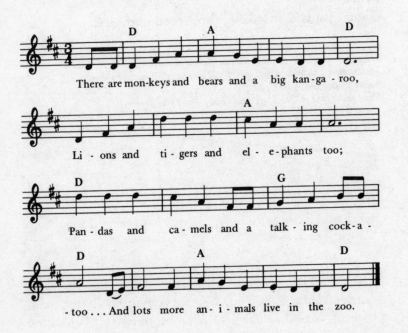

There are mon-keys and bears and a big kan-ga-roo,
Li - ons and ti - gers and el - e - phants too;
Pan - das and ca - mels and a talk - ing cock-a -
- too . . . And lots more an - i - mals live in the zoo.

Odd Animals

Little Rabbit Fou Fou
  Forefingers to head for ears.
Went running through the forest;
  Fingers 'run' on the floor,
He chased all the fieldmice,
And bopped them on the head.
  Bang one clenched fist on the other.

The adult says:
In the forest a good fairy saw what had happened and
she said, 'Little Rabbit Fou Fou, you *mustn't* chase the
fieldmice and bop them on the head. I'll give you three
more chances . . . and if you don't stop I'll turn YOU
into a fieldmouse!'

But . . .
Little Rabbit Fou Fou, etc.
  Repeat it all again until he has used up his three chances.

The good fairy saw what he was doing and she said,
'Little Rabbit Fou Fou, I gave you three chances and
you *still* chased all the fieldmice and bopped them on the
head. Now I'm going to turn *you* into a fieldmouse . . .'
and she *did*!

Now little Rabbit Fou Fou
Had a brother Chou Chou,
Who *also* chased the fieldmice
And bopped them on the head.

So little Rabbit Chou Chou
Chased his brother Fou Fou;
He thought *he* was a fieldmouse
And bopped *him* on the head!

The good fairy saw what he was doing, etc.

This can go on until everyone has had enough.
The verse is sung to the tune of Down by the Station, Early in the Morning
(see page 50).

An elephant goes like this and that,
Pat knees.
He's terribly big,
Hands high.
And he's terribly fat;
Hands wide.
He has no fingers,
Wriggle fingers.
And has no toes,
Touch toes.
But goodness gracious,
What a long nose!
Curl hand away from nose.

This can be sung to the tune for The Fisherman Rows his Boat Along (see page 258).

One grey elephant balancing
Step by step on a piece of string;
He thought it was such tremendous fun
He called for another elephant to come.

Two grey elephants balancing, etc.

Then:
Five grey elephants balancing
Step by step on a piece of string;
But all of a sudden the thin string broke . . .
And down came all those elephant folk!

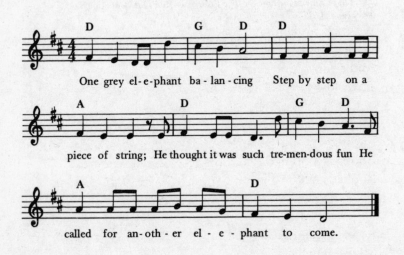

Another version of this is:

An elephant went out to play
Upon a spider's web one day;
He thought it such a tremendous stunt
That he called for another little elephant.

Two elephants went out to play, etc.

Down in the jungle where nobody goes,
There's a great big gorilla
Washing his clothes;
With a rub-a-dub here,
And a rub-a-dub there;
That's the way he washes his clothes!

Chorus:
Boobady boom–boom, boogie-woogie, woogie,
Boobady boom–boom, boogie-woogie, woogie;
Boobady boom–boom, boogie-woogie, woogie;
That's the way he washes his clothes!

Repeat for different animals, e.g.
Mouse (*tiny voice*)
Snake (*hissy voice*)
Elephant (*big slow voice*)

This can be sung to the tune Three Little Fishes and a Momma Fishie too.

Katie Beardie had a sheep,
She taught it to skip and leap;
Wasn't she a clever sheep?
Good old Katie Beardie!

Chorus:
Clap, clap, clap your hands,
Clap your hands along with us;
Clap, clap, clap your hands,
Going to the circus.

Then she had:
a frog . . . she taught it to jump on logs.
some mice . . . she taught them to skate on ice.
a pig . . . she taught it to dance a jig.
a worm . . . she taught it to do a juggling turn.

There was a wee lassie called Maggie,
Whose dog was ENORMOUS and shaggy;
The front end of him
Looked vicious and grim . . .
But the tail end was friendly and waggy!

The Slithergardee has crawled out of the sea,
He may catch all the others
But he won't catch me!
No – you won't catch me
Old Slithergardee;
You may catch all the others
But you won't . . . oops . . . Ow!

SHEL SILVERSTEIN

15 *Some Special People*

Old John Muddlecombe lost his cap.

Hands on head.

He couldn't find it anywhere, the poor old chap;

Look around, high, low for cap.

He walked down the High Street, and everybody said,

Walk round still looking under and round.

'Silly John Muddlecombe, you've got it on your
    HEAD!'

Chip-chop, chip-chop, Chipper Chopper Joe,
Chip-chop, chip-chop, Chipper Chopper Joe.
One big blow!
Ouch! my toe!
Chipper Chopper Joe chops wood just so!

*Children pretend to chop down trees, hop on one foot on the fourth line, then chop
again on the last line.*

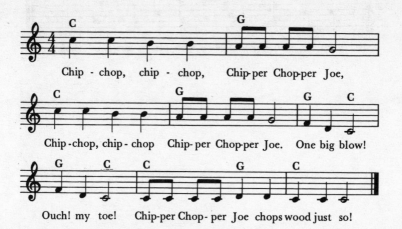

Cobbler, Cobbler, mend my shoe,
> *Hammer with fists on knees.*

Get it done by half-past two.

My toe is peeping through,
> *Drum feet on floor.*

Cobbler, Cobbler, mend my shoe.
> *Hammer with fists on knees.*

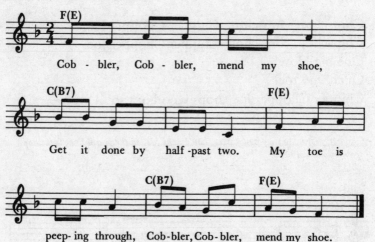

A sailor went to sea, sea, sea,
To see what he could see, see, see;
But all that he could see, see, see,
Was the bottom of the deep blue sea, sea, sea!

*This is used by older children as a skipping game or for handclapping. Small
children can manage a very simple handclapping sequence by clapping hands
together for each word, then each time they say 'sea' and 'see', patting their knees.
The next time around they can clap high, or low, or above their head, or on the
table, etc.*

Here comes Mrs Macaroni,
Riding on a big fat pony!
Here she comes in all her glory . . .
Mrs Macaroni!
Rum Tum Suzie-Anna,
Rum Tum Suzie-Anna,
Rum Tum Suzie-Anna,
Mrs Macaroni!

*'Mrs Macaroni' goes round the inside of the ring of children in the opposite
direction to the way they are moving. (Very small children can just sit in a ring.)
At the end of the verse she partners the child who is opposite to her and they dance
in the ring to the Rum Tum Suzi-Anna chorus. Then the chosen child becomes the
next Mrs Macaroni.
Sing this to the tune of Bobby Shafto.*

Yankee Doodle came to London
Riding on a pony;
He stuck a feather in his hat
And called it Macaroni!

Yankee Doodle Doodle Doo,
Yankee Doodle Dandy;
Yankee Doodle got it wrong,
The feather's made of candy!

Second verse ELIZABETH MATTERSON

Use the traditional tune.

If you should meet a giant,
Don't say, 'You're very tall!'
Or he might take you in his hand . . .
And say 'You're very SMALL!'

The Mystery Man has come to town,
Come to town, come to town;
He is walking up and down,
Up and down the street.

What has the Mystery Man for you?
Please put your hands behind you, do!
The Mystery Man he has a treat
For everyone he meets.

The 'Mystery Man' has a bag full of objects. He walks up and down the line or round the ring of sitting children. At the end of the first verse he stops by a child who puts his hand behind his back. An object from the bag is put in the child's hands and he has to guess what it is just by the feel of it. If he guesses correctly he becomes the next Mystery Man.
This is sung to the tune of There was a Princess Long Ago.

There was a man lived in the moon,
Lived in the moon, lived in the moon;
There was a man lived in the moon,
And his name was Aiken Drum!

His hat was made of cream cheese, etc.

His coat was made of roast beef, etc.

Follow these with verses about his trousers, shirt, socks, shoes, asking the children what each was made of . . . then finish with:
And he played upon a ladle, etc.
And his name was Aiken Drum!

Granny in the kitchen,
Doing a bit of stitching;
In came a bogy man
And chased Granny out!
'Oh,' said Granny,
'That's not fair.'
'Oh,' said the bogy man,
'I don't care!'

*This is another Irish version of the rhyme Piggy (Paddy) on the Railway
(see page 202).*

There were five great big Indians,
They stood so straight and tall;
They tried to fit in a little canoe
And one of them did fall!
SPLOSH!

There were four great big Indians, etc.

Then:
There were no great big Indians
Standing straight and tall;
They all got wet and ran off home . . .
And they got a TERRIBLE telling off from their
    mummy!
        Said with much head shaking.

                                        EMM et al.

*Use fingers of one hand for Indians and the other hand for the canoe.
This can be sung to the tune given for Five Little Spacemen (see page 295).*

There were five little spacemen
Going to the moon,
One stayed to close the door
And that left only four . . .So

There were four little spacemen
Going to the moon,
One stopped to make some tea
And that left only three . . .So

There were three little spacemen
Going to the moon,
One couldn't find his shoe
And that left only two . . .So

There were two little spacemen
Going to the moon,
One couldn't get his spacesuit on
And that left only one . . .Now

One little spaceman
Did go to the moon . . .
Then say:
Ten, Nine, eight, seven, six, five, four, three, two, one,
BLAST OFF!
But he didn't like it . . .
Shake head sadly.
And he came back quite soon!

BRENDA WEST and ELIZABETH MATTERSON

Capo 1st fret for chords in brackets

There were five lit-tle space-men Go-ing to the moon,

One stayed to close the door And that left on-ly four .. So

I know a man called Mr Red –
He wears saucepans on his head.
I know a man called Mr Black –
He keeps peanuts in a sack.
I know a man called Mr Pink –
He fell head first in the sink.
I know a man called Mr Blue –
He keeps white mice in his shoe.
I know a man called Mr Brown –
He rides tigers into town.
I know a man called Mr Green –
The nicest man I've ever seen!

*This can be a sort of response chant where one adult
says the first line and the children and other adults
say the second line.*

The poor King found a goldfish in his bath,
A goldfish in his bath, a goldfish in his bath;
The poor King found a goldfish in his bath,
It swam between his toes!

The poor King found a monkey in his soup, etc.
It pulled the poor King's beard!

The poor King found a crocodile on the stairs, etc.
It nipped the poor King's nose!

The poor King found a tiger in his bed, etc.
It ate the poor King up!

Words C. GREEN and music J. HOLDSTOCK

*For very small children it might be a good idea to ask them what they think
the tiger did.*

Capo 1st fret for chords in brackets

Once a man walked on my toes,
Along my legs up to my nose;
'Go away,' I said, and so he jumped . . .
Right on to my head!

Ask the children what else might walk on their toes.

There was a man who always wore
A saucepan on his head;
I asked him what he did it for . . .
'I don't know why,' he said,
'It always makes my ears so sore —
I *am* a foolish man . . .
I should have left it off before
And worn a frying-pan!'

CHRISTOPHER CHAMBERLAIN

Pip Pip Pippety Pip
Slid on the lino, Slippety Slip,
Fell down the stairs, Trippety Trip,
Tore her knickers, Rippety Rip;
Started to cry, Drippety Drip,
Poor little Pippa Pippety Pip!

SPIKE MILLIGAN

Sammy Smith would eat and drink
From morning until night;
He filled his mouth so full of meat
It was a dreadful sight! (*Ugh!*)
Indeed he ate and drank so fast,
And used to stuff and cram;
The name they called him by at last
Was greedy, GREEDY Sam!

Five tall soldiers standing in a row
     Hold up five fingers.
Waiting for their orders
Before they could go.
Along came the wind and blew off a hat,
     Blow hard.
So the soldier had to chase it . . .
     Run fingers along the floor.
What a shame,
     Shake head.
But that was that!
     Big shrug.

Four tall soldiers standing in a row, etc.

Then:
No tall soldiers standing in a row
Waiting for their orders
Before they could go
But the wind wasn't lonely
When the soldiers had gone . . .
He just played with all the hats,
And he had lots of fun!

EMM et al.

16 Singing and Dancing

Games

You put your right arm in,
You put your right arm out,
You put your right arm in
And you shake it all about!
You do the hokey-cokey
And you turn around . . .
That's what it's all about!

Do, do the hokey-cokey,
Do, do the hokey-cokey,
Do, do the hokey-cokey,
Knees bend, arms stretch,
Rah! Rah! Rah!

*Repeat with left arm, right leg, left leg, whole self . . . and any other bits of them
the children suggest. Just in case any adult cannot remember, the first verse is done
standing still in a ring and the hokey-cokey is done by lifting both neighbours' hands
high.*
*For the chorus the ring closes in, sweeping arms up high, and then retreats,
bringing arms low, for each of the first three lines. Smaller children who are just
getting the hang of this may prefer not to hold their neighbours' hands to start with,
especially if their neighbours are bigger and stronger than they are.*
Use the traditional tune.

There's a little sandy girl,
Sitting on a stone;
Crying, crying, because she's all alone.
Rise up, sandy girl,
Dry your tears away!
Choose the one you love the best
To come out to play.

The sandy girl, or boy (or to speed things up for very small children there can be two little sandy people), sits head in hands on a cushion in the middle of the ring of children who walk round singing the verse. She/he/they then choose a child from the ring to hold both hands and skip round on the spot while the tune is la-la-ed and clapped to again. The chosen child (children) then becomes the next to sit on the cushion.

Capo 1st fret for chords in brackets

Here we go Looby Lou,
Here we go Looby Light,
Here we go Looby Lou,
All on a Saturday night.

You put your right foot in,
You put your right foot out,
You shake it a little, a little,
And turn yourself about.

You put your left foot in, etc.

You put your right hand in, etc.

You put your left hand in, etc.

You put your whole self in, etc.

During the first verse the children skip round in a ring.
In the following verses they do the appropriate actions.
Use the traditional tune.
This is very similar to the hokey-cokey but as the children
do not have to join together younger children may find
this easier.

Skip, skip, skip to my lou,
Skip, skip, skip to my lou;
Skip, skip, skip to my lou,
Skip to my lou, my darling.

> *Each pair of children hold hands and skip round in a 'twizz',*
> *i.e. on the spot, not moving round the room.*

Cows in the meadow, moo, moo, moo . . . etc.

> *Pairs face each other, fingers to head for horns*
> *and nod to each other on moo, moo, moo.*

Skip, skip, skip to my lou, etc.
> *Repeat after each verse.*

Flies in the sugar bowl, shoo, shoo, shoo, etc.

> *Make shooing movement with hands towards partner on shoo, shoo, shoo.*

Train is a-coming, choo, choo, choo, etc.

> *One child is the driver and holds on to the 'engine' partner*
> *who moves his arms as they go round the room. Repeat this*
> *verse to reverse places so they each have a turn at being*
> *the engine.*

Somebody's hiding, boo, boo, boo, etc.

> *Hide faces with hands and 'boo' out at partners on*
> *boo, boo, boo.*

Somebody's tired, ooh, ooh, ooh, etc.

> *Children rest faces on hands, music slows up and at the*
> *end they sit/flop down with a big yawn.*

SUE WHITHAM and DOT PHILLIPS

This version of Skip to my Lou is useful for just an adult and a child, two children, twenty-two children or even fifty-two children if there is a big party. The only moving round the room is during the train verse and by this time they have got used to the rhythm and only move at the speed of the song. The chorus is repeated between each verse so it is quite a long game.

Skip, skip, skip to my lou, Skip, skip, skip to my lou;

Skip, skip, skip to my lou, Skip to my lou, my dar-ling.

In and out the dusty bluebells,
In and out the dusty bluebells,
In and out the dusty bluebells,
I shall be your master!

Tippety, tappety, on your shoulder,
Tippety, tappety, on your shoulder,
Tippety, tappety, on your shoulder,
I shall be your master!

The children make a ring holding hands, high enough to make arches. One child skips in and out during the first verse. For the second verse he taps the child nearest to him on the shoulder on each word until the verse stops. The last child to be tapped has to take the 'master' by the waist (in some versions a handkerchief links the two children) and follow him through the arches. The next time the second child does the tapping. The line of children going through the arches gets longer and as the ring consequently gets smaller it becomes more and more difficult to manoeuvre through the arches. Very small children may find this too much and the same game can be played with the first 'master' abdicating each time so that there are never more than two children going through the arches.

This is sung to the tune for Bobby Shafto.

Songs

She'll be coming round the mountain when she comes,
   Toot, Toot!
She'll be coming round the mountain when she comes,
   Toot, Toot!
She'll be coming round the mountain –
She'll be coming round the mountain –
She'll be coming round the mountain when she comes,
   Toot, Toot!

She'll be riding six white horses when she comes,
   Whoa back, etc.
(*On last line add:* Toot, Toot!)

And we'll all go out to meet her when she comes,
   Hi babe, etc.
(*On last line add:* Whoa back, Toot, Toot!)

And we'll kill the old red rooster when she comes,
   Chop, chop! etc.
(*On last line add:* Hi babe, Whoa back, Toot, Toot!)

And we'll all have chicken and dumplings when she
   comes, Yum, yum! etc.
(*On last line add:* Chop, chop, Hi babe, Whoa back,
Toot, Toot!)

Actions:

Toot, toot	*— pretend to pull the whistle-cord.*
Whoa back	*— pretend to pull on the reins.*
Hi babe	*— wave vigorously.*
Chop, chop	*— pretend to hold a chicken with one hand and chop at its neck with the other.*
Yum, yum	*— rub tummy.*

Use the traditional tune.

There was an old man called Michael Finnigin,
He grew whiskers on his chin-igin,
The wind came out and blew them in-igin,
Poor old Michael Finnigin . . .
Begin-igin!

There was an old man called Michael Finnigin,
He ate winkles off a pin-igin,
He grew fat and then grew thin-igin,
Poor old Michael Finnigin . . .
Begin-igin!

There was an old man called Michael Finnigin,
He went out and made a din-igin,
His neighbours came and threw him in-igin,
Poor old Michael Finnigin . . .
Begin-igin!

There are many more verses to this old song, but children are quite happy with just one or two. This can be used as a clapping song, clapping on every second beat. Older children may be able to keep two clapping rhythms going . . . half the group clap the timing of the words and the other half clap every second beat.

I know an old lady who swallowed a fly,
But I don't know why
She swallowed a fly . . .
I guess she'll die!

I know an old lady who swallowed a spider
That wriggled and wriggled and wriggled inside her;
She swallowed the spider to catch the fly
But I don't know why she swallowed a fly . . .
I guess she'll die!

I know an old lady who swallowed a cat,
Fancy that! She swallowed a cat!
She swallowed the cat to catch the spider
That wriggled and wriggled and wriggled inside her;
She swallowed the spider, etc.

I know an old lady who swallowed a dog,
What a hog! To swallow a dog!
She swallowed the dog to catch the cat,
Fancy that! She swallowed a cat!
She swallowed the cat, etc.

I know an old lady who swallowed a horse . . .
She's dead . . . of course!

ROSE BONNE

Ten green bottles, hanging on a wall,
Ten green bottles, hanging on a wall,
If one green bottle should accidentally fall,
There'll be nine green bottles
Hanging on the wall.

Nine green bottles, etc.

*This much-loved old song can be used in many different ways and with
different words. Once children have learned it it is one of the ones
they can keep going by themselves without adult help.*

We went to the Animal Fair,
All the birds and the beasts were there;
A big baboon by the light of the moon
Was combing his auburn hair.
The monkey tripped on a bump,
And slid down the elephant's trunk,
The elephant sneezed and fell on his knees . . .
And that was the end of the monkey
Monkey, monkey, monketty monk!

John Brown's baby has a cold upon his chest,
John Brown's baby has a cold upon his chest,
John Brown's baby has a cold upon his chest,
So we rubbed him with camphorated oil!

Camphor-amphor-amphor-ated,
Camphor-amphor-amphor-ated,
Camphor-amphor-amphor-ated,
So we rubbed him with camphorated oil!

The second time the verse is sung the word 'chest' is not sung . . .
instead the hands are tapped on the chest.
The third time the word 'cold' is not sung, instead everyone gives
a little cough.
The fourth time the word 'baby' is not sung, instead everyone folds
their arms and rocks them.
This is about as much as young children can manage. Older children
go on to miss out the John Brown's and clap instead.

Index of First Lines

Acknowledgements

Thanks are due to the following publishers and authors for permission to reproduce: 'Aeroplanes, aeroplanes, all in a row' by Linda Chesterman reprinted from *Music for the Nursery School* (George Harrap & Company Ltd, October 1935) by permission of the Harrap Publishing Group Ltd; 'Between the valley and the hill' by Rose Fyleman reprinted from *Speech Rhymes* by permission of A. & C. Black; 'Chick, chick, chick, chick, chicken' by Holt, McGhee, King copyright © Campbell, Connelly & Co. Ltd, 1925 by permission of Campbell, Connelly & Co. Ltd; 'Five little ducks went swimming one day' and 'A tiny, tiny worm' by Wyn Daniel Evans, 'This is the way we wash our clothes' by Lilian McCrea, 'Three jellyfish, three jellyfish' by Jean Chadwick all from *The Book of a Thousand Poems* edited by Clive Sansom, reproduced by kind permission of Unwin Hyman, a division of HarperCollins Publishers Ltd; 'Four scarlet berries' by Mary Vivian reprinted from *The Book of a Thousand Poems* by permission of Unwin Hyman Ltd; 'Heads and shoulders, knees and toes' by Linda Chesterman reprinted from *Music for the Nursery School* (George Harrap & Company Ltd, October 1935) by permission of the Harrap Publishing Group Ltd; 'How much is that doggie in the window?' by Bob Merrill, reproduced by permission of Warner Chappell Music Ltd; 'I had a little cherry stone' from *Nursery Rhymes and Finger Plays* (Pitman Publishing, 1941) by permission of Pitman Publishing; 'I'm a lion in the forest and I'm looking for my tea' by Barbara Ireson reprinted from *Over and Over Again* by Barbara Ireson and Christopher Rowe; 'Little Arabella Miller' by Ann Elliot reprinted from *Fingers and Thumbs* (Stainer & Bell Ltd, 1933) by permission of Stainer & Bell Ltd; 'Little Mary, looking wistful' by Max Fatchen reprinted from *Wry Rhymes for Troublesome Times* by Max Fatchen (Viking Kestrel, 1983) copyright © Max Fatchen, 1983; 'Little Pippa' by Spike Milligan copyright © Spike Milligan, 1963 reproduced from *The Pot Boiler* (Dobson) by permission of Spike Milligan Productions Ltd; 'The Milkman' by Clive Sansom, copyright © Clive Sansom, 1974 reproduced from *Speech Rhymes* (A. & C. Black) by permission of A. & C. Black (Publishers) Ltd; 'On the Bibblbonty Hill' by Rose Fyleman reprinted from *Widdy-Widdy-Wurkey* (Blackwell) reprinted by permission of A. & C. Black (Publishers) Ltd; 'Pussy cat, Pussy cat' by Max Fatchen (Viking Kestrel, 1983) copyright © Max Fatchen, 1983; 'Stop says the red light' and 'Stop! Look! and Think!' reprinted from Tufty Road Safety Scheme by permission of The National Tufty Club and The Royal Society for the Prevention of Accidents; 'The Teddy Bears' Picnic' by John Bratton and Jimmy Kennedy © 1907, M. Witmark and Sons, USA, B. Feldman & Co. Ltd, London WC2H 0EA/International Music Publishing, Essex IG8 8HN used by permission; 'There was a man who always wore' by Christopher Chamberlain reprinted from *Speech Rhymes* chosen by Clive Sansom by permission of A. & C. Black (Publishers) Ltd; 'Two fat gentlemen met in a lane' by Boyce and Bartlett reprinted from *Nursery Rhymes and Finger Plays* by Clive Sansom (Pitman Publishing, 1941) by permission of Pitman Publishing; 'Watch that truck' reprinted from Tufty Road Safety Scheme by permission of the National Tufty Club and The Royal Society for the Prevention of Accidents; 'Water in bottles, water in pans' by Rodney Bennett and Clive

Sansom reprinted from *Speech Rhymes* (1974) by permission of A. & C. Black (Publishers) Ltd; 'When all the cows were sleeping' copyright © Maecenas, Belwin Mills Music Ltd, London WC2H oEA/International Music Publishing, Essex 1G8 8HN, used by permission.

To those people who generously allowed their own original songs to be included: Diana Neal for 'All the little milk teeth'; Sheila Grove for 'Baby Peter, where are you?' and 'Two little eyes'; Elizabeth Bennett for 'Here we go round the Christmas tree', 'Diwali is here again', 'Curry and rice' and 'Chapatti in your hand'; Sue Browne and Elizabeth Matterson for 'Five mince pies'; Zelah Lockett for 'The shepherds sat around the fire'; Brenda West and Elizabeth Matterson for 'Walking out on Hallowe'en' and 'Five little spacemen'; Sue Whitham for 'It's the music box' and a new version of 'Skip, skip, skip to my lou'; Dot Phillips for 'Tambourine, tambourine how do you play?'; Patricia Sears for 'Copy, copy, copy me do!'; Yvonne Broadbent and Elizabeth Matterson for 'Ten little letters'; Katie Adamson for additional verses to 'Aeroplanes, aeroplanes'; Glenda Banks for additions to 'Hickory Dickory Dock' and 'Four little fishes'; and Barnstaple Children's Library and Elizabeth Matterson for 'Ten wiry sparklers'.

To all those people who, in the best tradition of passing on and adding to a good song, have contributed to the items labelled 'EMM et al.'.

To the following people and groups who 'passed on' some of the items which are new additions to *This Little Puffin* . . .: Nursery School Collections 1965 for 'Here we go round the Jingle Ring', 'I went to school one morning', 'Roly-poly pudding', 'She sailed away', 'Down by the river' and 'There's a little sandy girl'; Londonderry Nursery School for 'Foxy's creeping round the farm' and 'Katie Beardie had a sheep'; Love Lane School, IOW for 'Birthday candles on a cake'; Bluebell Valley Nursery School, Bristol for 'Cows in the kitchen'; Rosemary Nursery School, Bristol for the variation of 'Sing a song of sixpence'; Little Hayes Nursery School, Bristol for 'Pumpkin, pumpkin, round and fat', '"Splash," said a raindrop', 'Hippety Hop' and 'Poor little bird in a bamboo cage'; St Werbergh's Nursery School, Bristol for 'If you should meet a giant' and 'Sammy Smith'; The Lawns Nursery School, Windsor for the variation of 'Baa Baa black sheep', 'The Easter Bunny', 'I went to the kitchen', 'Five cherry cakes' and 'I know a man called Mr Red'; Hertsey Nursery School for 'A chubby little snowman'; Eastfield CI School Nursery, Louth for 'The fisherman rows his boat along'; Margaret Gray and the Belfast Nursery School teachers for 'My dolly has to stay in bed', 'In my house there is a room', 'Pitter, patter, pit, pat', 'My friend Sarah', 'The wheels on my bike', 'Come to the station', 'John Brown's tractor', 'The turkey is a funny bird', 'A hive for a honey-bee', 'I have a little spider', 'Row, boys, row', 'Little Tommy Tadpole' and 'Slippery Sam'; Alison Wells and family for 'Going fishing in the deep blue sea'; Rachel Wake's Grandma for 'She didn't dance'; Shirley Downs for 'Giddy up and away we go'; Joan Clayton for a variation on 'Baa Baa black sheep'; Christine Edwards for the play group version of 'Humpty Dumpty'; Marcella Stewart for 'Father Christmas, he got stuck' and 'Hello Peter, hello Adam'; Jean Freeman for 'Here we go up to Bethlehem'; Nicola Husk nds for 'I'm driving in my car'; Gill Osmond for 'If you're Rosie and you know it'; Julie Bull for 'There was a terrible collision', 'Seagull, seagull', 'Mr Smith the Keeper' and 'Lord Longleat had a game reserve';

Heather Brown and Margaret Scott for 'Five brown eggs'; Zelah Lockett for 'I saw a little blue-bird'; Diana Lowe for 'Mousie, Mousie'; Jean Evans for 'Old MacDonald had a shop'; Madge Bugden for 'One day we built a snowman' and 'Five small stars'; Nicola Pfaff for 'Mr Moon, you're up too soon'; Dora Johnston for 'Here comes Mrs Macaroni'; Sheila Grove for 'Once a man walked on my toes'; a play group parent for 'What did Mary do today?' and the play group Leaders for 'Wash your dirty hands', 'Edward Whitham, where are you?', 'Emma and Jo are in the ring', 'This old man, he played one' and 'Ten green bottles'.

To all the people, especially Joan Clayton, who helped to track down the origin of rhymes.

To the following people, organizations and publications who provided information and persuaded friends, relatives, members and readers to help with the research project: National Childbirth Trust; National Childminders' Association; Pre-School Play Groups Association; Scottish PPA; Orkneys PPA; Shetlands PPA; Northern Ireland PPA; Irish PPA; Save the Children Fund; MenCap; College of Speech Therapists; Children's Library Service, Belfast; IOW Nursery Teachers; IOW NCT members; CRS Records and Tapes; Nottingham Educational Supplies; Ray Lovely Music; *Parents* magazine; *Under Fives* magazine; *Young Mother* magazine; *Nursery World* magazine; *The Times Educational Supplement*; *Books for your Children*; *AFASIC* magazine and *Youth Library Review*.

A Space to Add Your Own Favourite Songs

It all started with a Scarecrow

Puffin is well over sixty years old.
Sounds ancient, doesn't it? But Puffin has never been
so lively. We're always on the lookout for the next big
idea, which is how it began all those years ago.

Penguin Books was a big idea from the mind of
a man called Allen Lane, who in 1935 invented
the quality paperback and changed the world.
**And from great Penguins, great Puffins grew,
changing the face of children's books forever.**

The first four Puffin Picture Books were hatched in 1940 and the
first Puffin story book featured a man with broomstick arms called
Worzel Gummidge. In 1967 Kaye Webb, Puffin Editor, started the
Puffin Club, promising to **'make children into readers'**.
She kept that promise and over 200,000 children became
devoted Puffineers through their quarterly instalments of
Puffin Post, which is now back for a new generation.

Many years from now, we hope you'll look back and
remember Puffin with a smile. **No matter what your age
or what you're into, there's a Puffin for everyone.**
The possibilities are endless, but one thing is for sure:
whether it's a picture book or a paperback, a sticker book
or a hardback, **if it's got that little Puffin
on it – it's bound to be good.**